Bloodrunner
Dragon

(Harper's Mountains, Book 1)

T. S. JOYCE

Bloodrunner Dragon

ISBN-13: 978-1533110633
ISBN-10: 1533110638
Copyright © 2016, T. S. Joyce
First electronic publication: April 2016

T. S. Joyce
www. tsjoyce.com

NOTE FROM THE AUTHOR:

This book is a work of fiction. The names, characters, places, and incidents are products of the writer's imagination or have been used fictitiously and are not to be construed as real. Any resemblance to persons, living or dead, actual events, locale or organizations is entirely coincidental. The author does not have any control over and does not assume any responsibility for third-party websites or their content.

Published in the United States of America

First digital publication: April 2016
First print publication: May 2016

Editing: Corinne DeMaagd
Cover Photography: Furious Fotog
Cover Model: Chase Ketron

DEDICATION

For you, my readers, my crew.
You have done more for me than you will ever know.
1010 is magic, and so are you.

ACKNOWLEDGMENTS

I couldn't write these books without my amazing team behind me. A huge thanks to Corinne DeMaagd, for helping me to polish my books, and for being an amazing and supportive friend. We've had a crazy adventure, haven't we, C? And to my husband, who is doing so much behind the scenes, and wanting no attention for it. He has always been there with me through my odd work hours, propping me up when I feel like I'm falling, and has the uncanny ability to understand when my characters are being unruly little beasties. Those are the days he has a stiff drink and a hug ready for me, and I wonder if he can actually read my mind. A huge thanks to Golden Czermak, for being such an incredible photog to work with on covers.

And last but never least, thank you to the crew, you, the reader, the reason I am able to do what I love. You let my books into your imaginations and for that, I can't tell you enough how much I appreciate you. Thank you for asking for each book in Damon's Mountains, and now for the books in Harper's Mountains. We are on this wild ride because of you.

ONE

The knock was always the same—delicate like a hummingbird. It was deceiving. That soft rasp on the door was the unassuming knock of a monster.

From where he sat, Wyatt James glared at the doorknob and hated the hole he'd dug himself into. He had no one to blame but himself, but that fact didn't settle the tremor of disgust in his stomach.

He could tell Arabella "no" this time. He could tell her to leave and never come to his cabin again, but then he would be right back to square one. He would be back to amounting to nothing.

Harper deserved better.

Stop it.

Wyatt swallowed the bile that crept up the back of his throat. He had no business thinking about her. Not here, and not now as the monster outside knocked politely again.

Clenching his fists, he stood slowly, then inhaled deeply to steady his pulse. Arabella would hear it. She would mistake his quickened heartbeat for fear. Arabella fed on fear. She would make it hurt worse.

She could save you, his inner bear snarled. *If you can't save yourself, Harper can.*

Wyatt gritted his teeth and threw open the door, careful to keep his eyes hollow. It hurt less if Arabella thought he was broken. Broken. He wanted to snort a laugh. No one could break him anymore.

Arabella was beautiful in that cold, hard Grecian-sculpture sort of way. She had perfect honey-colored curls that cascaded down her delicate shoulders. She wore a black, curve-fitting dress and burgundy lipstick. Her eyes were gray—a color he'd found striking on her in The Before.

Before he got desperate.

Before his bear went out of control.

Before he knew what Arabella was.

Now her eyes reminded him of the gray hue of a corpse. With a wicked smile, she canted her head and dragged her gaze down his face to his throat, then back up to his eyes. "You're thinking of her again."

Wyatt wanted to rip off her head. He wanted to tear her limb-from-limb for even talking about Harper. "Stay out of my head."

"You invited me into it," she whispered, stepping into his house and running a seductive hand up his chest. "Remember?"

Remembering hurt, though, so Wyatt winced away from the flashes that could bring him to his knees. Gripping her hand, he stopped her progress up his chest. She wasn't going to make him feel trapped. Not this time. "Let's get this over with."

"Mmmm." Arabella pouted. "No fun, Wyatt." She licked her lips and tossed him a fiery gaze, then let a wad of money fall from her fingertips to the table beside the door. "Don't forget that we both need each other, consort."

Consort. Wyatt swallowed hard and closed his eyes. He was the son of Tagan James, the long-running Alpha of the Ashe Crew. He harbored a dominant grizzly bear and wielded a power not even the humans understood, yet here he was, reduced to this—to nothing.

For Harper...

Arabella's teeth were like razors against his neck. She wasn't careful, but she didn't have to be. He had shifter healing. He wouldn't die easily. He wasn't some human she could drain and toss away. No, he was her chosen one. He was her prey. She'd hunted him for a long time so she could buy moments like this, when she would feed and know she was cowing a predator shifter. It was all about power for a woman like Arabella.

Wyatt linked his hands behind his head so he wouldn't touch her any more than necessary as she drank him up. God, it hurt. Every second dragged on for an hour. Her teeth were sharp, but she had a terrible habit of gnawing when she hit the veins just right. His hands grew cold behind his head, the tingling sensation flowing down to his palms, his wrists, his forearms.

"Enough," he murmured sternly.

His legs were feeling it now, too, the numbing sensation that came with the loss of so much blood. Arabella made a possessive hissing noise deep in her chest and clutched his neck, bit deeper.

Wyatt gripped her hair and yanked her backward. With as much hatred in his voice as he could muster, he gritted out, "Enough."

Arabella had that drunk look in her eyes as her pupils dilated. Her smile was tipsy as she wiped crimson off her lips. "So stingy, love."

"Don't call me that."

"Why not?"

Wyatt gave her a dead look and backed away slowly. "Because you don't know what love is." She never had and never would. She only knew fealty. She only knew what money could buy her.

Her bodyguards stood just outside the door, dressed in black three-piece suits, their hands clasped in front of their thighs, grim expressions on their pallid faces. "Careful," one of them murmured. "You'll hurt our queen's feelings."

Wyatt thought he saw the other guard smile, but perhaps he was mistaken. He'd come to learn monsters didn't have senses of humor.

Arabella sashayed out of his cabin, but turned on the porch, lips parted. Unable to listen to another word, Wyatt slammed the door.

The sound of Arabella's nails scratching down the wooden barrier that stood between them made his skin crawl.

Warmth trickled down his neck, and he let off a soft grunt as he pitched forward and landed on his balled-up fists and the toes of his boots. Blood made a sick pitter-pattering sound as it painted his dark wood floors red and trailed into the seam between planks. It wasn't the pain or loss of blood that made him retch. It was how dirty and used he felt. He couldn't force himself to look at the money on the table. Sure, it would help him establish a territory, and his bear needed it desperately, but no longer could he convince himself he was just donating his blood to help Arabella survive.

If he'd ever had a chance of winning Harper's heart, that had disappeared the day he sold his soul to the undead. Feeling like his heart was outside of his chest cavity, Wyatt let off a long snarl. He rested his forearms on the floor, buried his face in his hands, and screamed as loud, and as long, as he could.

He couldn't do this again. Couldn't risk his bear going on a bender. He was too close to town until he could afford his own territory. Wyatt staggered upward and strode for the bathroom. His reflection sickened him. Pale features, chest heaving, muscles tensed, eyes haunted, blood staining the neck of his shirt. If Harper saw him now, she wouldn't even recognize him from the boy she used to know. *Harper, Harper, Harper.* She deserved so much better than what he'd become.

His eyes lightened to an icy blue, the color that said his bear was right there, right under the surface. *She can save you*, his inner animal growled.

Wyatt slammed his fist into the mirror, shattering it into an intricate spiderweb. Fist throbbing, he turned on the tap as hot as it would go and cupped scalding water against his face and neck over and over to erase the filthy, clammy sensation Arabella's lips and teeth had left behind.

And when his throat finally stopped bleeding, when red stopped staining the porcelain white of the sink, when he felt like his bear wouldn't rip out of his skin as punishment for his weakness, Wyatt strode into the kitchen and pulled down the bottle of whisky. This was his "forget her" elixir. It was necessary on nights like this when Harper's memories were scratching at his mind.

He'd been good once. He'd been worthy of her, and now look at him. Consort to the Queen of the Asheville Coven. Nothing more than a blood-bag for a woman he hated. Wyatt took a long, deep drink of the whiskey and settled onto his couch, clenching and unclenching his cut-up fist.

Harper was suffering with The Unrest, and here he was, doing not-enough.

He pulled his cell phone from his back pocket and stared at her number, as he always did when he was struggling to keep from shattering. Perhaps she'd changed it years ago.

Just to see how it felt, Wyatt opened the message screen. He could call her and see her face when she answered before she realized it was him and hung up. Maybe if he just saw her, it would ease this spinning sensation he couldn't seem to get rid of.

But then she would see him. See how different he looked. She would see his unshaven face, his ruined neck, and his empty eyes, and she would know the boy she loved once was dead.

But it felt so good, sitting here pretending he could talk to her. So before he could change his mind, Wyatt punched in the words he'd wanted to say to her for the last ten years.

I miss you. I miss us. I miss who I was when I was with you.

It's getting cold outside.

And then, feeling utterly reckless and desperate to connect with something in this world...with someone...he hit send.

TWO

It's getting cold outside.

Harper had read the last part a hundred times over the last week. If she'd had any doubt who texted her from the unknown number, it had been laid to rest with *It's getting cold outside.*

That was the code she and Wyatt had used as kids when they needed to meet up at their secret spot to vent, cry, or later in their teens when they'd fallen hard into love, to hold each other.

But why now? Why had he reached out to her after all this time? Wyatt had done a bang-up job of ignoring her for an entire decade. He barely even talked to her when he came to visit the Ashe Crew for the holidays. In fact, he'd only spent a handful of days there since he'd blown out of town when he was eighteen.

Harper shook her head and frowned out the window of her rental car. Rain was pouring down into the parking lot of the local bar in Bryson City, North Carolina. Who in their right mind named the bar Drat's Boozehouse?

She sighed, and the sound tapered into a low rumble in her chest. Her dragon didn't like being cooped up, and sitting on a plane with a bunch of whiney humans all day had her wanting to make some ash. Harper stopped fidgeting with a loose thread on her sweater sleeve and pulled out the brown contact from her left eye. One quick glance in the mirror, and that was better. One brown eye, one blue, and the lighter one had a dragon's elongated pupil, proof of what dwelled inside of her.

She tracked a pair of bar-goers through the muddy parking lot. The man was holding his jacket over his date's head, protecting her from the downpour. It was sweet.

God, what was she doing here?

Wyatt had probably meant to send it to someone else. No, she could've convinced herself of that if he hadn't included the last sentence. He'd tacked that on because he'd wanted her to be certain it was him.

He missed her? He missed how he'd been when they were together? Did he even remember that far back? Harper did, but she'd assumed he'd deemed what they had a childhood crush and forgotten all about her.

She lifted her hand, palm flat, and screwed her face up at the shake she witnessed there. She was a motherfuckin' dragon shifter, and she had the tremors over a message from a man she didn't know anymore? Wyatt was a stranger who'd probably just got drunk and messaged her as a prank. Perhaps as a way to rip her up even more. As a way to tether her heart to him for another decade. Prick. Another rumble rattled from her chest. Wyatt was about to be a burnt prick.

A sudden urge to turn back around and catch the next flight out of North Carolina froze her against the seat. If she did this, if she tracked him down, she would knowingly put her heart right in front of him to trample again. He wasn't careful with other people's feelings. His father, Tagan, had told her time and time again it was because he had a dominant brawler bear inside of him, and he would settle when he was alpha someday. But she didn't buy it.

Wyatt had been a sweet boy once, until he wasn't.

A sudden humming took her chest, and she doubled over the vibration. She hated this—The Unrest. It made her feel sick, like she was going to Change. Like she would get stuck between her human form and her dragon and be trapped in here as *other*. It ruined her sleep and made it hard to keep food down, and sometimes it went on for so long she thought she would die from it. Not this time, though. This time, the humming stopped. She gasped for breath and relaxed against the squeaky leather of the seat.

She'd loved her dragon until The Unrest began.

As she got out of the rental, the rain felt good against her flushed face. She couldn't look like a drowned rat for Wyatt, though, so she hurried to the front door of Drat's. Inside, the walls were covered in vintage, neon beer lights and rusted-out, metal street signs. She wiped her feet on the mat only to nearly bust her ass in a puddle on the stained laminate flooring.

This was obviously the local hangout if the dirty looks and tight-knit groups of patrons were anything to go by. Perfect. Weston Novak, one of her childhood friends, had said the last he heard of Wyatt, he'd been living in some mountain hideaway near Bryson City, North Carolina. And if she was going to find him, this was her best shot at tracking him down in this small town. She'd bet her left tit Wyatt was a drinker now.

"S'cuse me," she said politely to a trio of beer-gutted stale-smelling humans. "Can you tell me if Wyatt James lives around here?"

"Who wants to know," the dark-headed one asked through a suspicious glare.

She pursed her lips to bite back her impatience. "My name is Harper. I know Wyatt from way back."

"Are you another one of them dragons?" he asked, twirling his finger in the general direction of her left eye.

"One round," a beefed-up muscle man slurred at the bartender. "Come on, Kane. One round, and if I win this one, you let us all have drinks on the house."

Ignoring the taunts Muscle Man was throwing to

the bartender, Harper offered Beergut an empty smile and excused herself. She wouldn't have any luck with shifter-haters.

As she approached the bar, the man behind lifted his chin and yelled, "I'm not playing with you tonight, Carl. No free drinks." He swung his gaze to Harper. "Except maybe for you." He ran a rag down the counter and cocked his head.

Out of habit, she scented the air, but he didn't smell of fur. Human. Her sense of smell might not be as good as a grizzly shifter, but she did all right.

"You passin' through?" he asked.

"Just here for a little visit. I have a f—" Her mouth still stuttered over that word. "Friend. I have a friend who lives here, and I'm looking for him."

The bartender had pitch black hair, shaved short on the sides and longer up top. A tendril of tattoo ink peeked out from under the long sleeve of his sweater. The black ink extended past his wrist and stretched down his hand to his knuckles, though she couldn't make out the design. He had chiseled cheekbones and faint dimples that probably deepened when he smiled. He looked about her age, maybe a little older, but his eyes were hidden behind a pair of sunglasses.

Perhaps he had vision problems. But when she shifted her weight on the barstool, his face turned with her. A fashion statement then.

"Nice eye," he said with an edge of something she didn't quite understand in his deep timbre.

"Thanks," she murmured, uncertain. "Do you know a Wyatt James?"

The bartender, Kane, poured a shot of whiskey and slid it over to her. "On me."

She narrowed her eyes thoughtfully, then tipped her head back and shot the burning liquor. Hissing at the sharp aftertaste, she set the empty glass down and asked again, "Do you know Wyatt James?"

"People around here are real protective of each other," Kane said, drying a glass slowly.

"I'm not here to hurt him."

"Surely you can understand my hesitation. I don't usually have shifters like you show up in this bar. You're a little dangerous for my taste, and if, theoretically, Wyatt did live around these parts, and if, theoretically, you tracked him down to his cabin in the woods, I'd feel mighty guilty if he turned up burnt to a crisp and in the belly of a Bloodrunner Dragon."

Harper froze. "How do you know that word?"

The corner of Kane's lip lifted in a feral snarl. "I know lots of things, Harper Keller. But I don't know any Wyatt James."

"See, lots of humans think we can tell a lie from the eyes, from the inability to hold our gaze and say the fib. Your voice gives your lie away, though."

"Or maybe I don't care if you catch me lying. I owe you nothing, Bloodrunner."

She swallowed down a growl. "Don't call me that. That's not a term for humans."

He set his dry glass on the countertop at the end of a row of clean ones "How about this?" he murmured in a dangerous voice. "How about you and I arm wrestle?"

Her face went completely slack. "What?"

"Arm wrestle me, Bloodrunner. If I win, you turn back around and leave my town the way you came."

Harper shook her leg in quick succession. She wanted to char this asshole for using the name of her ancient clan. "And if I win?"

"I'll point you in the general direction of Wyatt James."

Dumbass human, thinking he could best a shifter. "All right. Deal."

"Carl," Kane called, making his way from behind the bar. "This nice lady wants to arm wrestle me. If she wins, you can have your free round."

Carl swayed on his feet like a tranquilized bull. "Aw, man! She got skinny arms." He sat heavily into a chair, crossed his arms over his paunch, and pouted.

"But she has a dragon eye," Beergut called from a few tables down. "She's a match for Kane."

And then the betting started. Not well, because alcohol plus math equaled disaster, but some five dollar bills were handed around as Harper sat across the table from Kane.

Kane smiled an empty expression, then settled his elbow on the table and offered his hand. Gripping his warm palm, Harper blew out a steadying breath and nodded when he asked if she was ready. Beergut said, "Ready, steady, go," and Harper was shocked to her bones when she tried and failed to slam Kane's hand to the table.

He was strong. Inhumanly strong, and she scented the air again as she strained against him. No fur. A bird of prey shifter perhaps? Gritting her teeth, she growled a deep rumbling sound as the dragon surged with power inside of her, and at least now he looked like he was trying.

Kane's arm muscles strained against his sweater as she moved him closer to the table, but he countered and brought them back up to even again.

"What are you?" she gritted out, pushing with all her might against his hand.

Kane yanked his glasses off, revealing two blazing gold-green eyes, both of which had elongated pupils. "I'm a Blackwing."

Harper gasped, and he slammed her hand against the table. A Blackwing Dragon? No. No, no, no, Marcus's line didn't exist anymore. Harper's grandfather, Damon, had killed him. Only Bloodrunners remained.

She yanked her hand out of Kane's and stood so fast the chair behind her toppled backward.

"I win," he said through a hollow smile. "Now get out."

The small drunken crowd cheered and booed around them, but the sound was muffled compared to the volume of her pounding heartbeat. She rubbed her throbbing hand where he'd gripped her too hard and whispered, "Wyatt was mine once." Because Kane should know who she was. Not the Bloodrunner ancestry that ran through her veins, but the real her, the one who had loved Wyatt once upon a time.

Kane's face faltered, and some emotion slashed through his unnerving eyes too quickly for her to decipher before his mask of disdain was back in place again. "This place isn't what you think," he said. "You should go for your own safety."

Harper dared to hold his gaze for a few seconds more, then nodded and made her way to the door. She'd lost the bet, and she had to live with that. She'd underestimated Kane and let him surprise her into losing, and that was her fault. She was walking out of here with no clues on Wyatt because she'd let her guard down.

A Blackwing. She couldn't even wrap her head around that. Kane was an ancestor of one of the last immortal dragons, turned mortal in a war with her grandfather. His entire lineage was poison, and what the fuck was Wyatt doing living in a town where a Blackwing had set up territory? The Unrest doubled her over in the rain. The humming was so heavy in her chest it was hard to breathe. One minute of hell was all it took to snap her out of hating Kane's ancestor.

And when she sucked that beautiful oxygen back into her lungs, Kane was standing against her car, directly in front of her, arms crossed and head canted like he'd been standing there for the entire show. "Yours how?"

"What?" she rasped out.

"You said Wyatt was yours once. Yours how?"

She shook her head for a long time. How did she explain what they used to be without exposing the deep fissure in her heart? How did she tell it to this unfeeling Blackwing without her voice shaking? *Just say it.*

"How?" Kane demanded louder, his eyes flashing with impatience.

"He was everything to me. I wasn't the same to him."

Kane dipped his chin to his chest, but his eyes didn't leave her. "Fuck," he murmured. Scratching his forehead in what looked like a gesture of irritation, he stared off down the dark street and said, "You'll find Wyatt's cabin off Old Sycamore. Third drive on the right. He'll be into something you aren't ready for. You picked the wrong night to come for him. He won't be your everything anymore." Kane sauntered off toward the bar. "Try not to die tonight, Bloodrunner."

"So you can kill me yourself?"

Kane turned and walked backward with a cocky gait and a bright grin. "Something like that." And then he spun back around and disappeared inside.

Under the thick fabric of her sweater, Harper's arms were covered with gooseflesh. Kane might have done her a favor by telling her where Wyatt lived, but there was something very wrong about him. He felt dangerous and had her dragon clawing to escape her skin and defend herself.

Harper rubbed her arms, desperate to get warmth back into them, then got into her car and locked the doors.

Behind Kane's cocky smile was the devil in disguise.

And now Harper got the distinct feeling that the third drive on Old Sycamore was a trap.

THREE

The autumn leaves were turning, and if Harper was here for pleasure, she would take a moment to enjoy the vibrant reds and oranges illuminated by the occasional street light along the black asphalt road. As it stood now though, with her instincts kicked up, these woods looked haunted. Little tornadoes of dried leaves swirled around the street as she coasted by, and the creaking branches of the towering trees that lined the road arced across, creating a dark funnel for her to drive through.

The third drive on the right had a mailbox with the door hanging open and was stuffed with junk mail as though no one had checked it in weeks. The asphalt changed to dark gravel as she turned, her headlights shining on the thick woods. She imagined for a moment that she saw Wyatt's chestnut-colored bear through the trees, but when she stomped on the brake and scanned the forest, nothing was there.

She huffed a disgusted breath. How many times had she done that over the years? How many times had she imagined him near her? An embarrassing amount since her dragon couldn't let people go. She couldn't move on to protect her own heart. Instead, her dragon was fine wallowing in what-ifs. What if she had been good enough? What if the November of their eighteenth year had never happened? *It's getting cold outside.*

A wave of The Unrest washed through her, but was gone in an instant, and thank God for small blessings. She had to keep her head right now. So close. She was so close to Wyatt. He was home. She could feel that old pull from when they were kids, that old excitement.

She tamped it down and reminded herself he was a stranger. She didn't know him anymore, and he didn't know her.

26

Easing onto the gas, she gripped the steering wheel so hard it creaked in her clenched fists. Her windshield wipers scraped a wave of water off the glass, and that's when she saw something unfathomable.

The clearing, the small cabin, and the woods made sense. Harper leaned over the wheel as horror filled her. There was a man doubled over, on hands and knees in the mud. He was holding his throat as a trio of suited men with pale, glowing skin beat and kicked him. A woman dressed in figure-hugging black lace stood to the side, chin lifted high as she watched with a plastered smile on her crimson lips. Another man held an umbrella over her, protecting her from the raindrops. There were bats everywhere, swirling, circling, washing this way and that like billowing smoke.

When the man on the ground dragged his blazing blue gaze to Harper, a soft, pained sound wrenched from her throat. Wyatt.

Fury blasted through her veins, and a long, deep snarl rattled her chest. The nerves evaporated, her pulse steadied, and her middle heated with the molten lava that said her dragon was about to bring hell to earth.

Numbly, she kicked open the door and got out. The car was still running, and the headlights reflected strangely in Wyatt's eyes as he tried and failed to scream something at her. His fingers were dripping red as he clutched his throat.

"Hallooo," the woman in lace called. "Who do we have here?"

"It's time for you to leave," Harper said in a much calmer voice than she felt. Right now, her dragon was roaring inside of her, filling up her head with a death chant.

"Here is where I belong," the woman said, angling her face in an animalistic gesture. She wasn't baring her neck like she should've been right now, but instead, she was daring Harper to come for it. "Wyatt is mine to do with as I please. And this pleases me."

"Harper, leave." Wyatt nearly choked on the words, and his eyes were so raw. So pained.

Harper dragged her gaze to the woman in lace. "Final warning, bitch."

The woman lowered her chin and smiled a challenge. And then she disappeared into a plume of thick, dark smoke.

Harper's instincts blared the moment before pain slashed across the back of her neck, but she'd expected a dirty fight. Vampires were like that. No honor. Harper hunched inward, then let her dragon explode from her middle. She wasn't as big as her grandfather, but she had the fire. Stretching her wings, Harper leaped off the ground and pushed the blood-sucker down with the wind she created. More smoke, and the others were in the fight now. Good. Two clicks of her fire-starter, and she whooshed gas out of her middle. Fire rained down on the clearing, and magma dripped from her curled lips. She arched her back at the top of a gust of wind, coasted for a moment, and then dove for the fleeing vampires. They couldn't disappear completely. Not when she was in this form and could see heat registers, and cold. Corpses on the run, and she could see them blurring around the smallest one, hurrying their queen on, protecting her. Fucking vampires thought they ran the world after shifter rights were established. Harper would need wooden stakes to do permanent damage, but she could blister and char them, and it would take them weeks to heal from her dragon's fire.

She maneuvered through the trees, tucking her wings at tight places, working her way closer to the cold blue apparitions blurring, disappearing, reappearing a few yards away. She let off a roar to tell the woman in lace she had no power here. Not anymore.

One last stream of fire, and she heard it—the pained screech of an undead queen.

Harper's instincts urged her back to Wyatt in case one of the bloodsuckers had stayed behind to finish him off, so she caught a cool gust, stretched her wings wide, and blasted upward through a break in the trees. Bowing her back, she turned around and pushed against the currents, faster and faster until she could see it again—Wyatt's cabin.

He was there in the yard, but now he was as she'd imagined all those years. A rip-roaring chestnut grizzly bear was locked in a battle with one of the men who'd beaten him. Snarling, roaring, slashing with his dagger-like claws. His eyes were fierce, flashing a fiery blue, his muzzle snarled up in the promise of death.

There was the Wyatt she remembered.

She landed hard in his yard, her claws sinking into the mud as she made her way in a tight circle near the fight. Even injured, Wyatt could handle himself, and Harper wouldn't dare her fire this close to him.

Wyatt's arm snaked around the man in the soggy suit, and he tried to disappear, but the bear had him now. Rain pelted down, and a flash of lightning crackled across the sky, illuminating the splintered porch stairs. One long plank jutted upward, the end broken and sharp. Wyatt pulled the vamp from the thick smoke and slammed him down onto a long spike of wood with a sickening sound. The man's mouth opened in a scream of agony before his face fell away in ashes as fire flared up his body. And then he disappeared in a firework of sparks that covered the porch like tiny fireflies in the early spring.

A long, satisfied rumble filled Harper's chest, because yes, the beast in her required a boon for the blood Wyatt shed tonight. One down and the whole damned coven burned, so why was Wyatt looking over his massive shoulder with sparks of fury in his eyes?

With a warning click of her fire starter and a soft

hiss of pain, she shrank back into her human skin.

Wyatt followed suit, but he was shaking and smelled of rage. "You shouldn't have come!"

Harper huffed a shocked laugh and stepped back. He had some nerve. "I think you mean 'thank you.'"

"I'm not ready for this!"

She held her palms up. "For what?" she yelled, her voice echoing through the mountains.

Wyatt inhaled deeply, gritting his teeth as he held his bleeding neck. He angled away, and now she could see it. There was pain in his eyes that he'd been masking as anger. He dragged his gaze down her naked body and back up to her eyes. "I'm not ready for you to be here yet."

He turned to go inside, but she didn't miss the fact that he stepped carefully over the thin layer of ash that remained of the vampire he'd staked. Harper stood in the rain as he slammed the door behind him. Pools of water gathered in her outstretched palms as she stood there, completely and utterly baffled on what just happened.

Maybe she should leave.

No. She'd come this far and would never make sense of this battle if she didn't get answers from him now. Why the hell was a coven of vampires after him in the first place, and why was he facing them alone? Shifters didn't work like that. Wyatt should've been an alpha of a crew by now. If he was, his crew had failed him epically.

She'd let him go before without explanations, and it had tortured her. Not tonight. Tonight she needed answers.

Harper bit back a curse and strode for her rental car. She pulled her duffle bag from the back seat and shouldered it. On the porch, she dressed as fast as she could with shaking hands.

She was here, and just inside was the man who had enamored her since she was a kid. Memories of people were tricky. It was easy to forget the bad and hold the good on a pedestal. And Wyatt Andrew James had been too far up there for her to settle for another man since.

It was time to let him go.

She pushed the hem of her shirt over her jeans and shoved the door open. Inside, it was much warmer and would've been homey if it weren't for the disaster on the floor. His television lay face-up next to the fallen TV stand. Papers, books, broken glass, and shredded couch cushions littered the floor. Carefully, Harper righted a coat rack and hung the single jacket she found on the floor onto one of the pegs.

"Don't," Wyatt growled from the kitchen. His back was to her, and he was scrubbing his neck in the sink. Was he using soap? He was a shifter. Infection wasn't a possibility. Wyatt's shoulders tensed as he retched. "Fuck," he said shakily as he rested his forehead on his crossed arms on the counter.

His skin was too pale, and the jeans he'd pulled on hung loose around his hips, but he was still a massive man. So different from the boy she remembered. As he turned slowly, an accidental smile curved her lips.

"What?" he asked, his brows lowering into a frown.

"I just thought..." She shrugged helplessly. "This is so weird, speaking to you after all this time. Outside, when I saw you fighting that vampire, I thought for a moment I recognized you. Your eyes maybe. But standing here in the light...it's just strange seeing your eyes in this body." She gestured to him as her cheeks flushed with heat.

Wyatt straightened his spine and rested the heels of his hands behind him on the edge of the counter. It made the hard curves of his arms look even more massive. Wyatt wasn't a boy anymore. A slash of pain filled her. She'd missed everything.

His choice.

"Look at me," he murmured.

Harper closed her eyes for a moment, sighed, then blinked them open and dared to hold his gaze. The boyishness had left his face completely. Now it was all chiseled lines and facial scruff. His nose flared slightly, and when he swallowed, his Adam's apple dipped low into his muscular throat. His eyes were still the color of frost, and his dark hair was damp, spiked up from where he'd run his hand through it. Probably in frustration. He'd had that habit when he was a kid, too.

He shook his head, and Harper was helpless to decipher the look in his eyes now.

"This isn't how I planned this. It's not what I want."

"You messaged me. You sent our code. Are you really surprised I showed up here?"

"After everything? Yeah. Hell yeah, I'm

surprised."

She offered a pained smile. "Everything. That was a long time ago. Are you going to tell me why you are at war with a coven?"

"I'm not at war." Any softness that had been in his face disappeared when he snarled up his lip. "I'm their pet." His eyes tightened at the corners. "I'm not like you remembered."

"Yeah, a Blackwing Dragon named Kane said the same thing."

"Chhh." Wyatt shook his head and busied himself with righting a couple of chairs that had been toppled near the splintered kitchen table. "Kane is no one you have to worry about."

"Really? Because he seemed real put-off that I'm a Bloodrunner."

"He's put off by all dragons. Did he send you?"

"He told me where you live, yes."

Wyatt winced. "I'll fuckin' kill him."

"You'd rather bleed out for some vampire's entertainment than see me again?" She tried to sound strong, but the bitterness crept into her tone. "Why are you here, Wyatt?"

"What do you mean? I live here."

"Not here in this house. Why are you across the entire damned country from Damon's mountains? Why don't you have a crew under you? Why are you some coven's chew toy?"

"I told you I wasn't ready for you to see me yet!"

"Well now I can't leave!"

"You can and you will."

Harper blinked back the burning sensation in her eyes. "And leave you alone and vulnerable to a coven?"

"It was my choice, and I'm not alone. I have Kane."

"And where the fuck is he tonight? Huh, Wyatt? Where's your friend?"

"You don't understand what you're talking about."

"You have a fucking dragon here, and yet I come here and see you out in the rain, on your hands and knees—"

"I told you I wasn't ready for—"

"Bleeding from your neck where you allowed that woman at your throat. That's what this is, right?" Harper picked up a wad of cash off the table and chucked it at him.

37

"I told you I wasn't—"

"If you fucking say that again, I'll torch you. Ten years. You've had ten years, and all that time you denied me closure—"

"I don't want closure—"

"You took *choice* away from me, Wyatt. My shot at a treasure to satisfy my dragon? My shot at happiness? You stole that from me! Then you left me in Saratoga to pick up the pieces alone, and now you can't even give me a fucking 'thank you for saving my life just now'?"

"Because I'm not okay!" he roared. "My choice was taken, too! At least you had the Ashe Crew. At least you had the Gray Backs and the Boarlanders and your grandfather. At least you had friends. November was my fault, Harper. You were the victim, and I was the villain, and that month set the tone for my whole fucking life." His voice dipped to a raspy whisper. "I'm the villain."

She felt slapped. "Don't you dare take November for yourself. Half of that burden is mine."

Wyatt slammed the last chair onto its legs and hooked his hands on his hips. He shook his head, eyes locked on hers. She thought he was looking at her with disgust until he swayed on his feet and stumbled back a few steps, then propped himself against the countertop. His neck really did look shredded, not just from the fresh cuts, but from layers of scarring.

"Wyatt, what did you get yourself into?" she asked.

He shook in earnest now and looked like he might retch again, but his lips stayed sealed. Typical. He'd been stubborn as a boy, too. "You know that saying? That one about the road to hell being paved in good intentions?"

"What was your intention?"

He winced and avoided her gaze. "To save you."

FOUR

"I'm not some damsel in distress, Wyatt. I'm the damn dragon. Save me how?" Harper asked.

Wyatt couldn't look at her. Couldn't watch the moisture that had rimmed her eyes fall down her cheek. Couldn't accept the fact that here he was, hurting her again. He wasn't fucking ready. He was supposed to have his shit together when he saw her for the first time after so long. He was supposed to be a territory owner, away from the shadow of the coven, and maybe even recruiting for a crew member or two. But this? She'd come in at the moment he was hitting rock bottom.

"Save me how?" she repeated louder.

God, she was beautiful. He'd always known she would grow up a stunner, but Harper was an angel. Long, wavy dark hair that shone like silk in the light of his small home. Her lips were downturned and heartbroken, but even pursed in disappointment, they were full and drinkable. He'd imagined her taste a million times since he'd left Saratoga. And now she was here, smelling like anger and dragon's fire, her damp clothes clinging to her skin, her eyes exactly how he remembered. Wide and honest, so direct, bracketed by dark lashes. One soft brown iris and one that belonged to her dragon. Blue, with the reptilian pupil that said Harper was at the top of the food chain.

The way she'd gone after that coven tonight was a thing of beauty. She'd always been too loyal for her own good.

"Is this you shutting down again?" Harper asked in a defeated tone.

"I was trying to cut ties with the coven tonight." She should at least know he was trying to dig himself out of his personal hell-hole.

"Is that woman your...yours?"

Wyatt really was going to be sick if she didn't stop talking like that. "Arabella belongs to no one."

"And you?"

Wyatt wished he didn't have to answer. Wished he could disappear into a cloud of smoke like those asshole vamps, but Harper was looking at him, and he knew her. She wouldn't let him get away with pleading the fifth. Not anymore. "Before tonight, I was her consort."

Harper rubbed her eyes with her fingertips and sighed out a heart-wrenching sound. "You need to eat. And then you need to clean up your house and pack your bags."

"Can't. I'm in this." He rolled his eyes over the rafters of his cabin. "My bear is wanting to set up territory. I choose the Smokey Mountains."

"Well, un-choose them and convince your bear to come back to Damon's mountains. You can't be here alone."

Then stay. Stay with me. The question was there on the tip of his tongue, but she deserved better than a broken man who begged. She deserved him stronger. "Saratoga isn't my home anymore, Harper. There's too many shifters up there, too little territory.

There is nothing for me there."

"Except your family, Wyatt! Except your friends."
Anger sparked in her eyes. "Except. Me."

He huffed a breath and sank down on the couch.
Maybe the room would stop spinning. "Harper, you
and I both know you aren't mine. Beaston called it
from day one."

"No, he said I was destined to be with a great
alpha—"

"Exactly."

"You're so blind, Wyatt. You can't see the path
that is right in front of you. The path you threw
away."

"I'm trying to find it again!"

But Harper was good and done, and the only
answer she gave was the slamming of the door.

And then he was alone again.

Just like a villain deserved.

****

Wyatt was a dumbass, not a villain. She shut her
car door beside her and slammed her open palm
against the steering wheel until she felt better.

Oh, he was good. He'd trained himself to push
everyone away, but she wasn't easily moved

anymore. Okay, so Wyatt had listened to some prophecy and promptly exited her romantic life. Great. That was fine. She accepted it. His absence in her love life was his choice, not hers.

But everything in her said Wyatt needed a friend right now. Maybe not emotionally, but if he was going to survive the wrath of a coven, he needed numbers.

With a growl, she hit the speed dial of her cell and glared at Wyatt's cabin as it rang and rang. On the third chime, a familiar voice answered. "Hey, cuz."

Harper couldn't help the smile that stretched her lips. She always loved talking to Aaron. "Hey, remember that favor you owe me?"

"Yeees," he drawled suspiciously.

"I'm calling it in. Can you get some time off work?"

"Well, since my family name is on the damned fire house, yeah, I could take some R and R. Please tell me we're going somewhere tropical."

"I found Wyatt."

The line went silent. Several heartbeats later, Aaron asked, "Where?"

"North Carolina. He could use some friends right now."

"To sing kumbaya with?"

"Nah, something tells me he wouldn't be into that. You may want to bring your wooden stakes."

"Vampires?" She didn't miss the hint of excitement in his tone. Aaron Keller was a complete hellion with an inner grizzly that thrived on chaos.

"Yep."

A long, deep chuckle of glee resonated through the speaker. "Send me the address."

The line went dead, and Harper blew out a steadying breath before she hit the next number.

Aaron was always going to be the easy one.

The others were flight risks and would have to be lured in more carefully.

Two phone calls, a shit-ton of cursing and bullying, one feral roar to let one of the boys know she was serious, and an hour of pleading, and she was back to figuring out her next move.

Wyatt was fucked up.

It was more than the vampire who'd been gnawing at this neck, though that would be enough to break a proud man like him. There was something more going on here. He'd spoken of not being ready for closure, of trying to save her. He'd built a

45

mountain of secrets over the last decade, crawled up the pile of his mistakes, and there he sat, the King of Silence. The King of Nothing. That's not how she'd imagined his life would be.

Problem number one: Wyatt was alone.

Why the fuck was he alone? Even she could tell what kind of bear he harbored. He was so dominant it was hard to breathe around him, but he had zero submissive animals under him to keep him steady. Harper exhaled a pissed-off sigh and narrowed her eyes at his little cabin. Crews weren't just safety in numbers. They were affection and touch, which were so important to shifters to keep their animals sated. Loner shifters went mad. They took their own lives or were put down by alphas trying to protect humans.

Problem number two: Wyatt was sharing territory with a coven of angry vamps and one scary-as-hell Blackwing Dragon. Even if he was strong enough to live as a rogue, Wyatt wouldn't last long alone. Not surrounded by enemies like these. And Harper would be damned if she was going to leave here not knowing if she would ever see Wyatt alive again.

She shoved open her door and shouldered her

duffle bag again. It was too late to get a room at the bed and breakfast in town, and she wasn't sleeping in the car smack-dab in the middle of vamp-land.

Even the short walk to the cabin was creepy, just thinking about all those blood suckers. What would've happened to Wyatt if she hadn't shown up tonight? Chills blasted across her skin, and she hurried her steps so she could see him sooner. So she could remind herself he was still here, still breathing.

Some of the living room had been tidied, but only the single light in the kitchen was on. Most of the wreckage had been kicked into a pile near the front door. Long claw marks covered the surface of the couch cushions, and the stuffing had been ripped out. All that remained of her planned sleeping spot was the hard, cushion-less backing. Two springs had even breached the thin fabric. Nope.

The hiss of the shower was the only sound as she stepped carefully around piles of glass and into the single bedroom. Straight through was an ensuite bathroom with the light on that illuminated the small bedroom.

The bed was made, the furniture was sparse, and every rustic decoration was simple and in its place.

This told her the living room was all the vampires' doing and that Wyatt was just as tidy now as he was in his youth.

Harper quietly dressed for bed and pulled her toothbrush out of her bag. Silent as a hunter, she padded into the bathroom. The steam was really thick, as if Wyatt was scalding himself. A sick feeling filled her stomach as she realized what he was doing. Washing his neck out with soap made more sense now. His relationship with Arabella wasn't something he reveled in. He was disgusted. With himself or with Arabella, she didn't know yet. Maybe she didn't want to know. Maybe she wanted to hold onto her anger so she could keep her heart at a distance until he was okay for her to leave again.

Harper turned on the tap and squeezed some of Wyatt's toothpaste onto her brush.

The curtain was slapped aside, and Wyatt's startled face appeared, his eyes blazing such a light blue they were almost white. God, he'd turned out to be handsome.

He twitched his attention to her toothbrush, then back to her face. "What are you doing here? I thought you left."

"You thought wrong." Harper began brushing her teeth. From here, she could see a delicious sliver of his arm and right side. His abs sure made pretty shadows.

Wyatt's phone sat on the edge of the sink, and the screen lit up. A message from Kane came through.

"What does it say?" Wyatt asked, stretching his neck to see it.

"Are you still alive?" she read out loud around the froth of minty paste.

Harper picked it up and wrote back, *No thanks to you, Captain A-hole*. Send.

"What are you telling him?"

"I'm thanking him for being such an awesome friend," she muttered sarcastically as she created a cartoon penis and typed in, *You are a pecker and you suck at arm-wrestling*. Send.

Wyatt frowned and disappeared behind the curtain. A moment later, the water turned off.

"I usually shake off to dry," he muttered after a minute of silence.

Harper set the phone down, spat her toothpaste, and tried not to laugh. "Like a dog?"

"Can you hand me a towel."

49

"I already saw your dick tonight. Don't let me stop you from your routine shake-off."

"Yeah, well it feels weird now. Being naked when I'm pissed after a shift is really fuckin' different than stepping out of a shower."

Harper rinsed her mouth and dried her lips with the hand towel, then handed the tiny piece of fabric to him with a bright smile.

Wyatt narrowed his eyes at her offering. "I have a boner." He gave her a wicked grin and jacked up his eyebrow. "That wouldn't even cover it."

Harper threw the hand towel at his grinning face and sauntered out of the bathroom. She pulled down the thick cotton comforter of the bed, then snuggled under them. "My eyes are averted!"

The door closed with a decisive click, and Harper clasped her hands over her mouth to hide her laughter. God, she'd missed that naughty smile of his. It was just as she remembered. One side of his mouth curved up, and his eyes danced with a look that said he could find some trouble.

Harper fluffed up the pillows and surrounded herself with them, leaving him only one. Call her greedy, but she required a specific nest to sleep in, and she was pretty sure Wyatt wasn't going to complain about a line of barriers between them.

"Woman, get out of my bed."

"Polite decline. Your girlfriend shredded your couch cushions."

"I sleep naked."

He was trying to scare her off. Wouldn't work, though. "You can sleep one night with some pants on, or you can sleep on the floor. Now quit your bitchin' and pick a spot. I spent most of the day packed into a plane like a sardine with a bunch of complaining humans, spent an hour and a half driving here only to lose at arm wrestling to a friggin' Blackwing Dragon in a bar, and then battled vampires for you. I'm tired and not up for a row."

"You're bossier than I remember."

Harper smiled at the wall in the dark.

"And you're a pillow hog," he muttered as the bed bounced and bumped with him settling in.

When she looked over her shoulder, Wyatt was on top of the covers with his back to her. At least he was wearing briefs, but as he sighed in the dark, there was a slight tremble to his breath. He was going to freeze tonight.

Harper flopped over like a pancake. "I've decided something."

"I thought you were tired."

"I've decided we should be friends."

"That doesn't work for—"

"You don't have to argue about everything. We were friends for years before we were more. And I get it. We've both grown up and changed. But you need a friend right now, Wyatt." Harper hugged her pillow closer and thought of all she would endure with The Unrest. "And so do I."

Wyatt sighed in the dark. "Okay. Friends until you leave."

"No asshole. I mean...besties. We're gonna be BFFs. Messaging and meeting up around the holidays. Supporting each other when we settle down. Our kids will grow up knowing each other, and I'll be friends with the mate you choose. I want the whole nine."

"That's not the nine I want."

"Well, Wyatt," she said tiredly. "We did it your way for the last decade, and look where it landed us. I'm not asking for much. Just your friendship. You owe me."

Wyatt was shaking now...or shivering? On a

whim, Harper rested her hand on his taut back muscles. His skin was cold as ice. She hated Arabella. It should be the queen's ashes on the front porch right now. "Do you want to talk about it?"

"Talking doesn't help."

"You can talk or you can get under the covers."

A long snarl rattle Wyatt's chest, but after a few minutes, he slipped under the comforter.

"Night," she murmured.

"Night."

Minutes of silence dragged on, but just as her eyelids grew heavy, Wyatt asked, "Harper?"

"Yeah?"

"Thanks for…you know."

She didn't know. For coming here, or helping him fight the vampires? Was he thanking her for not leaving? He could mean any or all of it, but her answer was still the same. "Anytime."

FIVE

Harper cracked her eyes open and blinked against the early morning light that filtered through the single curtain-less window. Wyatt's arm was heavy across her hip, and his breath tickled the back of her neck. She took stock of her body. There were three pillows on the floor thrown up against the closet door, and the only remaining one was under her cheek. Sometime in the night, he'd mucked up her nest and chucked the pillows between them at the wall.

And that boner Wyatt joked about last night? He took morning wood to a whole new level. There was basically a tree trunk against her spine right now. His leg was thrown over hers, trapping her, and his forehead was resting against the back of her head. She could almost feel his lips on the back of her neck. Warmth pooled deep in her belly.

A hundred times they'd slept like this when they were kids when he would slip through her window late at night, or she would sneak out to the tree house they used to play in. He was a sleep cuddler. How could she have forgotten something so huge? Now the memories were so bright. She frowned. He needed affection, and so did his bear, so the reasons for him being rogue made even less sense now. He should've found a crew immediately after leaving Saratoga, but here he was, ten years later, still alone.

Wyatt let off a little sleep sound and rolled his hips against her back as he pulled her closer. But friends didn't let friends rub their boners on each other, so Harper wiggled out from under his grasp.

"Oh, my God, I'm sorry," he murmured in a hoarse voice. Wyatt sat straight up in bed as she rifled through her duffle bag. He scrubbed his hands down his facial scruff. "Look, I told you not to sleep in my bed. This is why I don't let women stay over."

Something green and ugly slithered around in her gut at the mention of other women, but she hid her face carefully and feigned an epic search for the pair of jeans at the bottom of her bag. Wyatt let off a muttered curse, and when she gave him her attention again, he was sitting on the edge of the bed, his back to her, running his hand through his hair slowly like he used to do when he was lost in thought. "This wasn't how I wanted to see you again."

"You said that last night."

"And I meant it. I had these plans. I wasn't supposed to be like this when you came here."

With a sigh, Harper sat on the bed, nice and far away from Sex Pot Wyatt.

His back muscles flexed with the movement of his hand over his hair, but something else caught her attention. He had bruising that stretched from his scarred neck all the way down his shoulder blade.

"Geez," she murmured, crawling over to him. She touched the purple discoloring softly, and Wyatt tensed.

She flinched away, but determined, she pressed her palm against his warm, bruised skin again. Wyatt blew out a long breath, and his tension seemed to disappear with it. He relaxed little by little under her hand. Slowly, Harper wrapped her arms around his middle and rested her cheek against the strong planes of his back. "Promise me you won't let her do this to you again."

Wyatt huffed a breath and shook his head. His hand slipped over hers, as if he wanted her to stay. "If it happens again, it won't be my choice."

She didn't miss that he'd denied her his promise, though.

He slipped out of her grasp and headed into the bathroom, then shut the door behind him, leaving Harper's arms tingling with a chill where he'd taken his warmth.

The Unrest took her so fast, she didn't have time to get away from the edge of the bed. The buzzing in her blood doubled her over and pain shot through her middle. She hit the ground beside the bed hard. She tucked her knees to her chest and stared at the blue bed skirt, desperate to stay awake. Sometimes it was bad like this.

"Harper!" Wyatt was holding her now, but his voice sounded so far away.

She felt like her hand was frozen around an

electric fence. Everything hurt. Every cell was exploding, every vein bursting, every muscle burning. *Can't breathe!*

Wyatt hugged her close and rested his cheek against hers. Lips against her ear, he said, "It's okay. I'm here." *I'm here.* A tear streamed from the corner of her eye as her body relaxed from the seizure.

Warmth trickled down her lip, and when she looked up, Wyatt didn't seem scared like she'd expected. He was calm. His eyes were subdued as though he'd been through a hundred of these with her.

He lifted her onto the bed and wrapped her up in the blanket, then strode into the bathroom. He came back with a damp rag and held it against her bleeding nose. Cradling her head in his lap, he rocked her gently. There was no call for an ambulance, no question, 'What's wrong?'

Suspicious, she whispered, "You know what this is?"

Wyatt wouldn't meet her gaze now. Instead, his attention stayed glued to the washcloth against her nose.

"Wyatt?" she gritted out.

"It's The Unrest." Heartbreak slashed through his eyes. "Your dragon didn't find her treasure. She never settled."

"How do you know that?"

Wyatt shook his head and didn't answer.

"How!"

"Because your grandfather told me."

No. This was her burden to bear. Her sickness. Pop-Pop hadn't gone through The Unrest. He'd been immortal most of his life and found his treasure a dozen times over in his eons on this earth. Her mother, Diem, hadn't gone through The Unrest because she had found her mate early. She'd found her treasure. This...this was Harper's shame, and her grandfather's betrayal felt like a slap against cold skin. "Why would he do that?"

Wyatt looked sick, and now his eyes were that blazing blue again. "Because Damon wanted to let me know it's my fault."

"That's not true."

"Isn't it?" The faint smell of rage wafted from Wyatt. "Beaston told me I would be the death of you, and now look. I failed to kill you the first time, and now you have The Unrest."

"Wyatt—"

"That's our fate, right?" His voice shook with fury. "Some people are born to hurt others, Harper. It's the way of things. It's how the world finds balance. There are good people and there are bad. From the moment I was born, I was meant to hurt you. And here you are, showing me kindness, despite the part I'm playing in your death."

Harper pushed off him. "You can't really believe that. You can't. We're all dying, Wyatt. From the day we're born, we're dying. That's the beauty of mortality. Every moment means something big because they are numbered. You got scared of what you could mean to me, so yeah, I guess in a way, this is your fault. Even if my destiny was to fall to The Unrest, I would've rather been happy while I had life left to live."

"I was trying to protect you—"

"You left to protect yourself! You left because shit got hard, Wyatt. You listened to Beaston's prophecy, you listened to my grandfather, and you listened to everyone but me. Me! I was right there saying you were mine, and you left."

She couldn't do this. Friendship wasn't going to

work—she still felt too deeply for him. Stupid dragon, killing herself for love.

Harper's breath hitched and her face crumpled. She would have to leave because she couldn't stay here and hurt this badly. But she should say how she felt in case she never got another chance because she and Wyatt were both headed to hell fast. "When I lost her—"

"I can't do this." Wyatt stood in a rush and paced the other side of the bed, pulled on a gray T-shirt like he needed something to do other than look at Harper. "I don't want to talk about her."

"You have to."

"I don't. Can't." The room was heavy with dominance and smelled of fur.

"I wanted her—"

"I fucked up, Harper! I fucked up. Beaston told me to be careful with you, and I wasn't. I should've used a condom every time, but I would lose my head around you. I couldn't afford to do that. Not when every damned female dragon dies to bear young! My young." Wyatt's face fell, and his eyes rimmed with moisture. "She was mine, and she was going to kill you. Janey was mine, and she was the reason you were going to die."

Harper ran the collar of her shirt over her wet cheeks and let off a pitiful sob. "She was beautiful."

"Stop."

"You should've looked at her! You should've been in Saratoga, visiting her grave with me, but you left me alone with all that hurt. I wanted her, Wyatt. I wanted her more than anything."

"You were eighteen, and you were going to die for a baby."

"Not just a baby. Our baby. Janey was *ours*." Harper rested her back against the closet door and sighed. "I might have lived. Damon picked my birth grandmother carefully, and my mom had a twenty-five-percent chance of surviving. She said my chances were better. Fifty-percent maybe."

Wyatt hooked his hands on his hips and shook his head, stared out the window. His jaw clenched so hard his muscles jumped there. "Fifty percent chance that I would lose you forever."

Harper wiped her eyes again. "No, Wyatt. A fifty percent chance that I could've given you everything. I keep thinking what if I'd been able to keep her. I imagine us sometimes. Up in Saratoga with Janey, happy, a family. You would be logging with one of the crews, and I would have my law practice in town, and Janey would be growing up with the other kids in Damon's mountains. The Unrest isn't your fault, Wyatt. It's mine for not being able to get her to air. You gave me my treasure when I was eighteen, and I couldn't take care of it. Couldn't protect it. I failed us. You reacted. I forgive you for everything. I just wanted to say that before I go. I forgive you."

Wyatt was to her in an instant, hugging her so tight it was hard to breathe, and she didn't even care about the discomfort. This right here, this moment, was the first thing that had felt real since the day he'd left.

"It wasn't your fault. You did everything right. She just wasn't meant to be ours, Harper. God needed her more."

A pained keening sound wrenched up her throat as she clutched onto his shirt and dampened the fabric with her tears. "That's all I needed to hear. That's all. This whole time, that's all I needed to hear from you."

Hugging her tighter, Wyatt's shoulders shook, and his breath hitched. His unshaven jaw rasped roughly against her cheek as he gave her the affection she'd pined for. The affection bear shifters gave better than any other shifter. He switched sides and ran his cheek across her other one.

Wyatt gripped the back of her head and pulled her face against his strong chest. And when he lowered his lips to her ear, he whispered salvation. "We've both punished ourselves for long enough. It's through."

It's through. Harper wrapped her arms around his neck and allowed him to pull her up off the ground. His words had blasted apart the big red ball of ache in her middle. She huffed a thick laugh at how relieved she felt. This...this was like flying. It was like cinder blocks being cut from her ankles and breaking the surface of the water. It was breathing again.

She closed her eyes tightly and stroked the back of his head as her dragon let off a long, relieved rattle. One day with him, and she was practically purring. Did her forgiveness make her weak? She didn't know. All she knew is that she'd bonded with Wyatt when she was young, and the tension of that bond had never gone away. She used to hate her dragon for holding onto him so tightly, but now Harper had to trust her. She had to. For whatever time she had left, she wanted to be happy.

And no person on the planet had ever, or would ever, make her happier than Wyatt.

SIX

Wyatt slammed the ax down on another log and shoved the split pieces into the pile next to the chopping block.

He was smiling like a dope, but that couldn't be helped. Harper was back in his life.

Okay, so maybe she wasn't his, never would be again and not like he wished, but at least they would get through the grit from the past. At least they could forgive each other and themselves, and right about now, it felt like a billion pounds of dead weight had lifted off his shoulders. Damn. He sucked in an easy drag of air. He couldn't even remember feeling this free.

Chop.

So now the real work would begin. She'd scared him with that seizure, and from what Damon said, it would only get worse if she didn't connect with something big. He had to push hard and find her dragon something to tether her to this world.

Chop.

Too bad he was about a hundred thousand dollars short. He squinted up at the mountains in the distance. His plan wouldn't have ever worked. Not at the pace he was earning money. He had shifts up at the gem mine, excavating dirt for tourists. It paid pretty well, and he'd been saving like mad for the past three years. From the second Damon had called him about Harper's first bout of sickness, he'd gone to work, but he hadn't realized she was this deep into The Unrest already.

Harper's bloody nose meant she was nearing her end and Wyatt's timeline had just been blown to hell.

Chop.

His funds from the coven had been cut off completely with the stunt he'd pulled last night. Arabella had tried for a more intimate approach to bleeding him, and he'd lost his mind and tried his damndest to put the leg of the kitchen chair through her chest cavity. He'd been making a thousand dollars a blood donation, but now he was back to only paychecks from the mine. It wasn't enough.

He lifted the ax to slam it back down onto the log he'd balanced on the block, but he paused as the throaty rumble of an engine rattled to him on the breeze.

Harper's silver rental car sat in his yard. It was broad daylight so the vamps were down in their dark basements. The only other person who'd ever come visit him here was Kane, but only once. They weren't the sitting-on-the-porch-drinking-lemonade type of friends. More like two predators living in the same territory who respected each other's boundaries. So who the fuck was driving the beefed-up, glossy black motorcycle up his gravel drive right now?

A tall man pulled the bike into Wyatt's yard and cut the engine, hit the kickstand with his giant black boot, and pulled his helmet and sunglasses off.

"Holy shit. Aaron?" He hadn't seen Aaron Keller in years.

Aaron gave him a toothy grin and nodded like

hell-yeah. He got off the bike and caught Wyatt's hug. Aaron clapped him on the back hard enough to shake his lungs loose, and Wyatt got overwhelmed with emotion. God, his bear had been falling apart since Harper had barreled back into his life last night. He gripped Aaron's navy sweater and opened his mouth to apologize for the scent of sadness he was putting off right now. But Aaron rested his forehead on top of Wyatt's shoulder and gripped the back of his head. He just stood there like that, embracing him like they used to when they were boys and hadn't seen each other in too damn long.

Wyatt inhaled sharply, trying to keep his shit together, but truth be told, his bear needed this. He needed touch, and Wyatt had been stupid to deprive his animal side of comradery for all this time. Wyatt leaned his cheek against Aaron's head and just was.

"I missed you, man," Aaron murmured. "You didn't just leave her. You left me, too."

Shit, shit, shit. Wyatt swallowed hard, over and over, and clenched Aaron's shirt harder. "I'm sorry."

Aaron gripped the back of his neck painfully hard, then released him and slung his arm over his shoulder. This was so strange. The Aaron of his memories was a lanky boy who looked downright emaciated next to the other men in the Breck Crew. He'd hit his grizzly growth spurts and now was a dominant bruin with at least seventy extra pounds of muscle on his frame. Tattoos peeked out from under the edge of his sleeves, and he had blond facial hair, only a couple shades darker than the hair on his head. He had piercings and ink and was built like a tank, and Wyatt was having a damn hard time meshing the way Aaron looked now with the memory he had of him.

Aaron beamed. "You should see your face right now. You look like you're seein' a ghost."

Wyatt laughed. "I am. I'm looking at the ghost of the kid I used to know. I'm gonna call you Roid Rage from here on."

Aaron shoved him hard and shadow boxed with him for a minute. "Yeah, well, you don't look the same either. You been hittin' the weights?"

"No," they both said at the same time and laughed. Bear shifters didn't have to spend time in the gym. They just had to feed their bodies plenty of red meat.

"Other than that, though, you look like shit,"

Aaron said, blond brows arched high. He jerked his chin toward Wyatt's neck. "You been feedin' vamps?"

"Long story."

"Which you will tell me because I'm gonna be here for a while."

"What do you mean?"

"I heard you're fighting vamps...I want in. I'm bored out of my mind in Breckenridge. It's like an ice cream social every other day, and I know all the girls there."

"Oh, yeah? And they aren't putting up with your shit anymore?"

"Exactly." Cupping his hand around his mouth, Aaron greeted his cousin with a bellowing, "Harper!"

Harper stood on the broken porch, leaning against the post with a mushy smile on her face as though she'd seen their entire exchange.

Aaron pointed to the soggy pile of ash in the distinct shape of a man on the broken stairs "Gross." He hopped over and lifted his cousin into the air, squeezing until she giggled.

To Harper, Wyatt mouthed, *Did you do this?*

Those sexy lips of hers curved up even higher as she nodded. Huh.

71

More rumbling sounded from down the road, and son of a gun, what now? Wyatt was already damn near weeping like a twelve-year-old girl at a boyband concert.

Two jacked-up Chevy's raced up the driveway toward them, zigzagging through the woods when the road got too thin for both. Someone was laughing like a psycho out their open window, and Wyatt squinted at the heavy tint to try and figure out who was driving.

The gunmetal gray truck skidded into the yard first, rooster-tailing mud until it rocked to a stop in front of the other one.

"You cheated, you mother fucker!" That voice was sort of familiar, but deeper.

Two slamming doors echoed through the clearing, and two more ghosts from Wyatt's past strode up to him, both of them looking like a pair of body builders jacked up on protein.

Ryder's hair was redder and his freckles darker than Wyatt remembered from the last time he saw him. And when the strutting giant grinned right before he pulled Wyatt into a hug that nearly killed him, he looked nothing shy of feral. He picked Wyatt up off the ground and drove him backward, whacking him on the back hard enough to sound like the snaps of a whip.

"This guy," Ryder said, dropping him abruptly and shoving Wyatt back to arms' length. "Fucking North Carolina? That's where you were hiding this whole time?"

"For the last few years, yeah. Man, the last time I saw you, you were nothin' but a scrawny pipsqueak," Wyatt said in disbelief.

"I growed up," Ryder joked.

"Yeah, but is all this necessary for a snowy owl shifter," Wyatt said, whacking him on the stony chest.

"Nah, but the ladies love it. I need to have a pretty lure if I want to catch the pretty fishes."

"Really?" Harper muttered from behind them.

"Have you ever been fishing in your life?" Aaron asked. "That's not at all how it works."

"Aaron!" Ryder called out. "Damn, Harper's calling the riffraff in." He bolted up onto the porch toward a chuckling Aaron.

Wyatt blew out a breath before he turned to Weston. He'd been the only one who had come and found Wyatt after he'd left. Maybe the others had tried, he didn't know, but Weston was the best tracker Wyatt had ever known. And for years, the Novak Raven had it in his head that he was gonna bring Wyatt back to Saratoga. They hadn't parted well on their last encounter.

Weston had a camouflage baseball cap covering his jet black hair, and his eyes were darkened from their normal green to the bottomless black of his inner raven. He wasn't smiling like the others. Instead, he stood there with his arms crossed over his chest and his face angled, exposing his neck. Wyatt hated that. It was his formal way of respecting Wyatt's dominant bear, but he wished it was an easier greeting, like the others had given him. He understood, though. This tension was on him.

"I'm here because Harper asked me to be." Weston offered his hand for a shake, then yanked Wyatt forward. "Hurt her again, and I'll fucking kill you."

"Noted," Wyatt gritted out, pulling his hand from Weston's and putting space between them.

"Wes," Harper warned. "He's made his apologies to me. We're okay."

"Yeah, well, you were always the forgiving one,

Harper. Don't mean the rest of us are the same."

"Let's get drunk and kill shit," Aaron said.

Ryder's hand shot in the air. "Yes, I want to do that."

"By 'kill shit' do you mean stake vampires?" Harper asked.

"Uh, yeah," Aaron said with a shrug and a baffled expression, like Harper should understand their man-language by now.

Wyatt swallowed his laugh, but mostly for Weston's benefit since he was still glaring at him.

"Harper, tell me you didn't get a mom-wagon for your rental car," Ryder demanded, his face all puckered up at her ride.

"Don't judge me, bird. It was all they had."

Ryder sure looked judgmental. "You traded your diesel truck for that shit?"

"You drive a truck now?" Wyatt asked. She'd driven one of those little pastel-colored slug-bugs when she was in high school, solar-powered flower bobble-head included.

"There's about a million things you don't know about me now, James," she said through a cocky grin. When they were kids, she had used his last name when she was flirting with him. Oooh, he wanted to suck that bottom lip until she said his first name again.

Weston shoved him hard, and Wyatt had to catch his balance. "Why are you starin' at her like she's a steak. She ain't yours anymore. Cut that shit out, or I'm leaving."

"Weeees," Ryder drawled, eyes rolled heavenward. "Chill out, man. Our Queen Sky Lizard has that same dopey look in her eyes."

"I really hate when you call me a sky lizard," Harper muttered.

"I saw a bar on the way in." With a grin Aaron said, "I can drive us."

"Yeah, let's see how many idiots can pile on the back of your bike," Wyatt said. "I'll drive."

"Are you designated driver tonight?" Ryder asked, waggling his eyebrows.

"Might as well be. My liver could use the break."

"Bender James, back at it again," Ryder crowed as he sauntered toward Wyatt's black F-150 parked on the side of the house.

"Bender James?" Wyatt asked, confused as everyone followed Ryder.

"You partied hard when we were teenagers," Harper explained as she walked past him. "At least your nickname isn't Sky Lizard."

Well, there was that. Shaking his head at the strange turn his life had taken in the last couple of days, Wyatt pulled his keys from his back pocket and jogged to catch up with the others.

And as he pulled out of the yard, Ryder opened the window and whooped. And then he yelled into the beyond, "The band is back together!"

"Temporarily," Weston muttered under his breath in the back.

But when Wyatt looked over at Harper, he was stunned by the moment. There was an easy smile on her lips as she watched the others, and her giggle was so damn beautiful. When she stuck her hand out the window and caught the breeze between her fingers, her eyes twinkled with happiness. Her dark hair floated this way and that, and when she looked at him, he didn't know how he'd done it. How had he gone this long without seeing her smile like this? How had he survived away from her infectious joy? Harper was so different from anyone he'd ever met. She'd always been to-the-death loyal, strong, and clear-headed. Every decision she made was quick, but right. She had been the glue of their group when they were kids, and now look at her. Even grown, she was still the glue.

After what he'd done, Harper had still hugged him and broke him back into a shape he recognized. She'd brought his friends back, and even if it was only for a short time, he wasn't going to take a minute of this for granted.

With a grin, he hit the gas and took the truck off-road through the fresh mud. Ryder and Aaron hung out the window, yelling sounds of pure happiness, and Wyatt knew he wasn't alone in how damn good this felt to be back together.

When Harper yelped and slid closer to him to avoid the splash of mud outside the window, he snaked his arm around her shoulders and kissed her hairline quick.

She grinned up at him, her shoulders shaking with a laugh. She bit his arm playfully and murmured, "You're welcome," as if she could tell his affection was a thank you.

From this moment on, no matter what happened, Wyatt was going to be better. He was going to work hard and long to be anything Harper wanted him to be. He was going to work to earn Weston's respect again and to deserve the embraces Ryder and Aaron had given him.

He wasn't where he wanted to be, but he was going to get there. They deserved the effort, because even if they left tomorrow, these people right here were his crew.

SEVEN

Harper was two drinks shy of three sheets to the wind.

It had been a long time since she'd cut loose, so perhaps she should slow it down a little. Especially since Wyatt was staying true to his word and drinking water.

He smiled for the tenth time in five minutes, and Harper's heart rate hadn't settled since he'd kissed her forehead in his truck. She'd expected it to feel like old times if he pressed his lips against her, but it hadn't. It had felt like new times. Like a new adventure, a new crush, with a new man. The miniature dragons fluttering around in her stomach were proof that she was in deep mud, and sinking deeper with every smile he gave her.

Ryder had his arm over Wyatt's shoulder, and they were talking non-stop, laughing, teasing each other. The hollow-eyed haunted Wyatt from last night was just a memory, and thank goodness for that. The boy she remembered wasn't gone...he'd just been a little lost.

"What's your end game?" Weston asked from right beside her.

Harper startled hard. No one could sneak up on a person like Weston. "What do you mean?"

Weston took a swig of his beer and narrowed his eyes at Wyatt. "Are you really going to forgive him for leaving us like he did? Are you really going to just move on with him like the last ten years didn't happen? I watched you pine for him, Harper. I was there watching you hurt. I was there when you started The Unrest. I was there waiting for you to purge him from your system, but you never did."

"Wait." Harper closed her eyes and shook her head, trying to sober up. "Do you...like me?"

"You mean would I like to fuck you? Sure. As

friends."

Harper frowned so hard her head started to hurt. "Do people do that? Fuck as friends?"

"Probably. But if you're asking me if I want to date you, no. You're one of my best friends, which is why I feel all protective of you. I don't want you to spend your whole life stuck in the past."

"Look, whatever happened with you and Wyatt, I'm sorry for it. That won't affect my decision to be his friend, Wes. He needs us."

Weston clicked his tongue against his teeth and sighed.

"Do you trust me?" she asked.

"Yeah. I wouldn't be here if I didn't," he uttered in a monotone.

"I appreciate you worrying over me, but I'm a grown woman, and I don't have a ton of time left."

Weston jerked his head to her and frowned. "Don't talk like that, Harper. It's not funny."

She smiled sadly. "Wouldn't joke about something like that."

"You'll be fine. Your dragon is just acting out because of the stuff you've been through. She'll get over it."

"The nosebleeds have started."

Weston downed his beer, set the empty bottle down too hard, and gestured to Kane for another.

Ignore her all he wanted, but he couldn't deny the facts. "Okay, what does your dad say?"

Weston's dad was a mystic with a sight that extended beyond the veil, beyond this realm. He was also one bad motherfucker with a monster grizzly in him. Beaston was never wrong in his visions.

Weston shook his head for a long time and finally said, "My dad isn't always right, you know. Not everything he says can be taken at face value."

Harper sucked down half her margarita and sighed. "That sounds like some fragrant bullshit to me, Wes. I want to be happy." She nudged him in the arm. "Tonight I'm happy, and you and Aaron and Ryder are a part of that. But him"—she gestured to Wyatt—"he's a big part of it, too. Let me keep my happy and don't make me feel weak for wanting it."

Weston gripped the back of her neck and pressed his forehead against hers. He closed his eyes and inhaled deeply, then released her and nodded to Aaron.

Thoughtfully, Harper watched them walk toward

a trio of pool tables along the back wall. Ryder was now asking Kane why he was wearing sunglasses inside, and she had the distinct feeling that dragon was going to get Ryder talking in circles, so she scooted over to the barstool right next to Wyatt. "Hey stranger."

"I'm a stranger now, am I? I guess that's fair."

"Do you still eat your pizza crust-first?"

His sexy smile reached his eyes, so blue and clear. "I do."

"Do you still play guitar?"

"I do not. I haven't picked one up since I left Saratoga."

"Pity."

"You always liked guitar players."

"Did you have lots of girlfriends?" She shouldn't have asked that, but she couldn't help her tipsy tongue.

Wyatt took a drink of his bottled water, and when he set it down, the smile had faded from his lips. "Don't do this."

"How many?"

Wyatt's gaze drifted to the pool table, and he ran his hands down his whiskers. "Two. I was a shitty boyfriend, though, and they didn't last long."

Did you love them? Did you compare them to me? Did you come close to claiming either of them? All the questions piled up, but she was too chicken to ask, so instead, Harper finished off her margarita and asked Kane for another.

"I liked your text last night," Kane said as he poured the tequila. "I figured it was you who responded."

"How'd you figure that," she slurred.

Kane grinned. His dark hair fell forward, covering his glasses as he squeezed a lime into her drink. "Because Wyatt's never sent me a dick-pic before."

"Wait, what?" Wyatt asked, pulling his phone from his back pocket.

"It was a cartoon dick," Harper said. "And furthermore I have dated, like, a million boys."

"Boys or men?" Kane asked.

"Stay out of it," she groused.

"A million is a lot," Wyatt said, and now anger flashed through his eyes like lightning. "I told you I don't want to do this. I don't want to know."

"Age twenty, I dated Laith Ingram, and we

French kissed. A lot."

"Cut her off," Wyatt growled out.

Kane grinned brightly and shoved the margarita toward Harper. "I like this side of your girl."

"She isn't—"

"Don't you fucking not-claim me in front of your friend, or I will burn all the hair off your stupid body."

Kane snorted, Harper slurped at her drink, Wyatt smelled like fur, and everything was great.

With a gulp, she said, "Age twenty-three, I had a one-night stand."

"Stop it." Hooo, Wyatt was making the air all heavy.

"I did because I was lonely and I wanted someone to touch me and make me feel good like you used to."

"This is awesome," Kane said popping a handful of peanuts from one of the community snack bowls into his mouth.

"Don't you have drinks to serve, man?" Wyatt asked.

"I think his name was Benjamin, and I almost let him eat me out, but then I changed my mind, and newsflash, he was a sloppy kisser. That night I learned what whiskey dick is, so I came out of there feeling really sexy. It was age twenty-five until I tried that one again, with more success, and I felt like a goddess until about five minutes later when I got sick to my stomach because he wasn't you." Harper hiccupped. "Age twenty-six, two weeks after my birthday, I had my first seizure."

The smile faded from Kane's lips. Good.

"I had my first bout of The Unrest, so I got scared. Terrified actually. I tried to find you. Wes wouldn't help me track you, and I hated everyone, my dragon especially because she was doing this to me. And then Derek Hoover, the man I dated out of desperation to save myself, cheated on me with anyone who had a slimy vagina hole."

"Whoa," Ryder said from Wyatt's other side.

Wyatt looked green and wouldn't meet her gaze anymore.

"So there is the million people I dated. Tell me about *Trixie-Nips* and *Cinnamon*."

Wyatt hung his head and heaved a sigh that tapered into a growl. "Trixie-Nips and Cinnamon were really named Ashley and Emma, and we broke up because they weren't you."

"He said your name when he fucked 'em," Kane said. "Both of them broke up with him in under two weeks. Came in here complaining to me like I could fix him."

"What the fuck, man?" Wyatt griped. "Piss off! Please, go literally anywhere but here."

"I'm helping."

"You're really not."

"Actually, he is." Harper smiled sheepishly. "That does make me feel better."

"Great," Wyatt gritted out. He chugged his water and crumpled the empty plastic bottle in his fist like he wished it was Kane's neck. He chucked the bottle at Kane, who caught it easily, and then Wyatt strode out of the bar without looking back.

"Woman," Ryder said, staring at the door as it slammed closed, "you sure know how to push them buttons." He yanked her half empty drink away. "You really are cut off."

"Don't tell me what to do."

"Sloppy," he said, shaking his head. He was smiling, though, so she shoved him in the arm before she meandered toward the door.

"You gonna make out with Wyatt?" Aaron called

across the whole damned bar.

"No!" Probably not. Just in case, though, she snatched a handful of peppermints from the jar by the door and dropped three trying to unwrap one.

"That's a yes," Aaron said as he leaned down to hit another ball into the side pocket.

Weston was watching her with a troubled mother-hen expression, but whatever. She was sotally tober. Sober. Totally sober.

Harper shoved open the exit door and promptly tripped over a rock on the sidewalk. With a yelp, she went down hard, but a few centimeters before her palms hit the ground, a pair of strong arms yanked her backward.

She flopped around in Wyatt's embrace and grinned up at him. At least, she thought she was grinning. Her lips were numb from the tequila. "My knight in shining camo."

Wyatt looked down at his camouflage-print thermal sweater and snorted. Setting her upright, he muttered, "You make it really hard to stay angry. I forgot about that part."

"We always sucked at fighting."

Wyatt's eyes were still blazing the color of frost,

but he ran his hand over his hair, mussing it as he tried and failed to contain a grin. "I don't think I've ever seen you drunk before."

"I'm not drunk." The peppermint flopped out of her mouth and hit the ground. Gritting her teeth in concentration, Harper swayed and reached for the candy. "Five second rule," she mumbled, but Wyatt kicked her sugary target into the street.

"Five second rules don't count when you drop something sticky in the dirt. It had a leaf on it, Harper."

Harper rocked her head all the way back and frowned. "You look grossed out. And tall. What are you now? Seven foot eleven inches?"

Wyatt huffed a laugh and shook his head. "That's a really specific number, and no. I'm six-three. I should probably get you home."

"Home. Your home?"

Wyatt cleared his throat, and a troubled frown marred his perfect face. "Yeah, my home. That's what I meant."

Harper looked at the peppermint in the street, all caked in mud now. "Well...I was going to seduce you, and now the boys will make fun of me. They'll think I couldn't close the deal."

"Close the—woman, what did you think was going to happen?"

"Making-out at the minimum, and maximum, banging in the parking lot. Maybe over there"—she pointed—"where it's all dark and romantic."

Wyatt looked up at the dark sky like he was praying for patience, but she could still see it there— that little smile. "First off, the parking lot of Drat's isn't romantic in any way, and you should really lift those standards, Harper. Second, you're wasted—"

"Tipsy—"

"And when I do make a move on you, I want you to remember it. As it stands now, I don't think you'll remember this conversation tomorrow, much less a quickie fuck in the parking lot, and where are your shoes?"

Harper looked down at her bare feet. Damn, her pedicure still looked foxy. But really, where were her flip flops? She looked around, trying to desperately remember where, and why, she took them off.

"Okay, don't worry," Wyatt said in that manly sexy voice of his. "They're probably still inside. I'll grab them and some water for you. I'll round up the boys while I'm at it."

As he disappeared inside, Harper murmured, "But I'm not thirsty." For water. She was definitely thirsty for Wyatt's lips. She'd been thinking about them non-stop since he pecked her on the head earlier. And now she was completely inebriated on the sexy smiles he'd been casting her way all night. Those and tequila.

The wind kicked up, and goosebumps rose in waves across her arms despite the warm sweater she wore. Dragon shifters ran hot, hence the comfort with flip-flops on this chilly autumn night. The world was fuzzy as she scanned the parking lot and narrowed her eyes at the trees that lined the street beyond. The leaves and limbs were perfectly still, but it was so windy near her that dust from the parking lot lifted in little cyclones.

And then she heard it. The *squeak, squeak* of bats.

With a gasp, she bolted for the door, and just as her fingertips brushed the handle, she was blasted backward. She was thrown into a tornado of chaos as she spun and fought. Harper hit the side of a truck with a deafening crash and then was pinned there against the mangled metal. *Dragon!* Where the fuck was she? Slashing pain stung her arms as she blocked punches too fast to be human. A long hiss filled her head as something cold wrapped around her neck.

Change, Change, Change!

Harper gasped for breath as the smoke solidified into Arabella, surrounded by her guards, her hand wrapped unwaveringly around Harper's throat. Too drunk. Harper was too drunk to summon the dragon. But she could still blow fire if she could suck in enough air to set off her fire-starter.

"You took my toy from me," Arabella rasped out in an icy voice that bounced around inside of Harper's head, each word echoing and overlapping. The side of Arabella's face was melted like metal warped in a fire from where Harper had burned her last night. Her gray eyes turned cold and dead in the moment before she opened her mouth, exposing razor sharp fangs, and sank her teeth into Harper's neck.

Harper clawed at the vampire's wrists to try and loosen her grip and thrashed as the outer edges of her vision collapsed inward. She scrabbled and kicked against the truck behind her, and then in desperation, she socked Arabella with a balled fist over and over. It was like punching a stony cliff face. The crack of Harper's bones was loud as pain seared up her arm.

There was chaos behind Arabella now. Fighting. Bats. Thick purple smoke. Ryder. Weston. Aaron was Changed into his grizzly bear and laying waste to everyone in his way. Not fast enough. *Help me!*

"Harper!" Weston screamed, his veins bulging in his neck as he fought the smoke and tried to reach her.

It wasn't enough. Not enough time. Not fair. Frost crept through her veins as Arabella drained her. *Please Dragon. Where are you?*

Like an apparition, Wyatt appeared through the smoke, his eyes white as snow and promising death, his teeth bared.

Beside him, the bats solidified into a vampire, but Wyatt grabbed him by the throat before he was solid and threw him with mesmerizing force.

"Wyatt!" someone yelled. Kane?

Like a spear, a pool stick came straight for Harper's face, but Wyatt caught it without looking, and in one smooth, blurred motion, he cracked it across his knee and rammed one jagged end into Arabella's back.

Arabella jerked backward, and her grip around Harper's throat loosened. Her crimson lips formed a silent screech of pain and shock as fire blazed up her body. And in an explosion of sparks, the Queen of the Asheville Coven collapsed in a pile of pungent ashes.

Harper fell forward, but Wyatt was there, holding her, telling her, "Breathe, baby. Just breathe."

Harper dragged air into her crushed windpipe. The adrenaline in her system had burned off most of the alcohol, and she could see everything so clearly now. The splintered, scorched pool stick in the middle of the ashes. The bats and smoke fleeing the parking lot and blending in with the darkness beyond. Aaron's blond grizzly pacing between a row of cars, his eyes wild and his neck torn open. Weston and Ryder, chests heaving, staring at her like she was already dead.

Kane was standing near the bar in the thinning smoke, but as she tried to thank him for helping her, he spat on the gravel and disappeared inside. A sob escaped her as she clutched to Wyatt's sweater and sucked sweet air.

Her dragon was here now, too big, violent, wanting more death because she was scared. Because she hadn't been able to wake up in time. Stupid tequila. Stupid. "I didn't know," Harper chanted over and over just for something to say. Just to hear her own voice and convince herself she was still alive.

"It's okay. Everything's okay," Wyatt said in a gravelly voice. But he had eased back enough to look at her throat with an expression that said he wanted more death as recompense, too.

"Wes," Wyatt said low. "Her hand."

"Yeah," Weston said, lifting her ruined fingers gingerly. It hurt so bad, like someone had shoved her arm into a fire.

His eyes were the pitch black of his raven's when he lifted them to Harper's. "This'll hurt."

"Do it," she gritted out. Waiting and mentally preparing wouldn't work. It would only make it worse. Shifter healing was fast. Too fast sometimes for broken pieces.

Wyatt pushed his weight against her, pinning her to the side of his dented truck. And just as she let out a scream at the pain of Weston resetting her bones, Wyatt kissed her, hard.

It wasn't the sweet kisses from when they were kids, or the passionate ones they learned about when they were old enough for intimacy. This one was fear and anger and loss all wrapped up into one breathtaking instant. Weston was done, and tears of pain streamed out the corners of her eyes, but Wyatt didn't release her. His lips softened, and he moved them slowly against hers, drinking her in until the pain eased and Harper went limp with exhaustion in his arms.

Wyatt bit her bottom lip gently, then disengaged and rested his forehead on hers. His breath was shaking, just like hers, and his eyes were closed tightly. And now she wanted to cry for reasons other than pain. She'd never thought she would get a chance to be held by him again, much less kissed. And it felt so good, so right. His lips were like a homecoming after a long trip.

Her cheeks heated with shame. "My dragon wasn't there."

"I know. It's okay." Wyatt folded her into his arms and strode around the back of his truck, the others following slowly.

"Aaron, Change back," Wyatt clipped out. "We

need to leave."

A grunt of pain sounded from behind them, and Harper looked around Wyatt's wide shoulder to see Aaron limping after them, holding his torn neck together. *I'm okay*, he mouthed.

That was close. Too close. She could've lost so much tonight.

Ryder yanked open the passenger door, and Wyatt set her inside, buckled her quickly while the boys piled in the back. And when Wyatt was behind the wheel, he slammed the door, revved the engine, and gunned it out of the parking lot as sirens sounded in the distance.

The law wasn't lenient on shifters. It never had been, not since they'd established rights over twenty years ago. No damage had been done except for Wyatt's dented truck and the final death of the Queen of the Asheville Coven. Law enforcement should give Wyatt a damned trophy for making the area safer from her fangs, but they wouldn't. They would cage him if they figured out what had happened in the parking lot of Drat's. Vampires had secured their rights like shifters had. Regardless of how long a vampire had lived, or what evil deeds they'd done in the shadows, a death was a death to the police.

The air was too heavy in here, and when Harper looked in the back seat, Weston was pulling off his shirt. He wadded it up and pressed it against her bitten neck, staunching the warm wetness that had been trickling from the wound.

Ryder had his face buried in his hands, and Aaron was naked from his shift, staring out the window with a haunted look.

And Wyatt...Harper wanted to hold his hand to silently tell him she was okay, but he felt so heavy right now she couldn't move an inch closer to him.

"Cut it out, man," Aaron muttered.

Wyatt didn't answer. The only sound was the acceleration as he hit the gas on a straightaway.

"Wyatt!" Aaron yelled. "I said cut that shit out or I'm going to Change again!"

Wyatt snarled a feral sound. When he tossed Aaron a shut-the-fuck-up glare over his shoulder, his eyes weren't human at all.

"I couldn't find my animal. I'm sorry," Harper murmured. Her skin was cold, but on the inside, she was burning. Maybe she was in shock.

"It was the alcohol," Wyatt growled out. "And

you're a fucking dragon, Harper. Stop apologizing."

Weston adjusted his shirt on her neck, applied more pressure. "You shouldn't have left her unprotected."

"He was going back in for my shoes," Harper said. "It's not his fault."

"Bullshit!" Weston barked out. "This is all his fault."

"Wes," Ryder drawled, relaxing back against the seat. "Cut him some slack."

"Why the fuck should I? Wyatt, you disappeared. You bolted. You pushed us all away for all these years, and do you know who you hurt the most by that?"

Wyatt twitched his chin and winced, like Weston's words physically burned him.

"Harper!" Weston bellowed.

"He's made his apologies," Harper murmured.

But Weston wasn't done. Not by a long shot. "You got her pregnant. You almost killed her. You almost took her away from all of us! And then you ran and did even more damage. You gave her The Unrest, Wyatt! You! She bonded to you. You were her fucking treasure, and you ditched her."

"Weston!" Harper yelled, yanking his shirt from underneath his hand just to make him stop touching her. He was speaking about personal things that he didn't understand. "That's enough."

"And then you bring her here and force her into some fucked-up war with the vamps. That's what this is, right? We just killed the queen of a coven. *The queen*. And I saw that look in her eyes, Wyatt. That vamp wanted to kill Harper. And judging from the scars on your neck, I'd say that's on you, too." Weston rammed himself backward against the seat and crossed his arms. "We should've never come here."

Such pain slashed across Wyatt's face, Harper couldn't bear to look at him. Couldn't bear to see the heartbreak there.

He swallowed audibly. "You're right, Wes. I've fucked up my whole life, and it hurt Harper. It hurt you and the people back home. I hurt everyone I care about. But I want to be better. I need to be."

Ryder leaned forward and gripped Wyatt's shoulder, shook him gently, then relaxed back against his seat.

"Why couldn't you just leave him alone, Harper?" Weston asked so softly she almost missed it.

She bit her lip and stalled on answering because, if she was honest with him, Wes might hate her. Not because he was jaded, but because he'd always worried over her. But if she didn't draw her line in the sand and tell them exactly where she stood, they would never really get it. None of them would.

She gave a helpless shrug. "Because I love him." She didn't dare look at Wyatt when she admitted that out loud, though she could feel him glance over at her.

Weston huffed a disappointed sound. "Bad choice, Harper."

Harper wrapped her arms around her middle and rested her cheek against the headrest, stared out at the night woods that lined the road. "You're wrong, Weston."

"Yeah? About what?"

She tossed a sad smile to Wyatt's faint reflection in the window. "You're wrong about love being a choice."

EIGHT

Harper massaged her palm with the thumb of her other hand. It still tingled from where her bones had healed. It would probably feel sore for a few days, but Weston was good. The crew he was born into, the Gray Backs, were notorious for fighting each other. Bone-setting was a skill they all possessed.

She touched her lips as she remembered the kiss Wyatt had given her against his truck. Nothing in her entire life had felt bigger. Perhaps it was because of the moment he had chosen, when she was in pain and in need of a beautiful distraction, when her emotions were soaring, and she was so relieved to still be breathing. Maybe it was because of that.

But more likely, that kiss had felt completely consuming because it was Wyatt, and she'd been suffering away from him. Her dragon felt whole in that moment, like nothing could break them apart again.

But as much as she wanted to bury herself in the shadow of safety Wyatt cast, she had a life away from here. She worked for her grandfather as his in-house lawyer. She had family and friends in Saratoga. There, things were easy and comfortable, while here, over the course of thirty hours, she'd experienced every emotion imaginable. Dragons weren't built for that. They were steady-eddy and cool, calm, collected. Swinging emotions got people burned and the earth scorched. Her ancestors had waged war on each other and killed off nearly every single immortal dragon. Now, only mortal halflings like her walked the earth. Maybe that's why she'd always struggled to fit in. She'd had a law practice down in Saratoga for a couple of years before she accepted the position overseeing all legal documentation pertaining to Pop-Pop's businesses. And in that two years, she'd made an effort to find something outside of Damon's mountains. She'd made friends, but as hard as she tried to build lasting bonds with the humans she spent time with, she was always *other*. She'd started wearing a brown contact over her dragon eye so people would stop staring and so she didn't have to smell their fear anymore.

And then Derek had come along, and she'd thought maybe he was the one she was supposed to find. She didn't feel as passionately about him as Wyatt, but he had been there for her, up until the day she saw him in the local coffee shop sucking on some skank's earlobe right there for everyone to see. She, Harper Keller, dragon-shifter, lawyer, powerhouse...hadn't been good enough. She, Harper Keller, vessel for The Unrest, displaced shifter, confused soul...had come in second to the trail of Derek's mistresses that drifted out of the woodwork after that.

She'd closed down her practice, let go of the relationships with the humans she'd been grasping at, and went back to the mountains where she almost belonged.

Everything had been perfect before Wyatt had left. Everything. It was home, little league baseball games on the weekends, school, family, crews, and safety. She could fly everywhere and never worry about being judged. But when she'd given up on Saratoga and gone back to the mountains, the air she flew felt different. Colder. Empty. The joy was gone because Wyatt's bear wasn't strolling the evergreen woods below her anymore.

And now she was here, and all those feelings were flooding back. All those memories. Shifting in the woods with the boys, Wyatt always let her Change first so he could watch her dragon emerge. Birthday parties with all the crews, treehouse rendezvous, Friday nights helping her surrogate mother, Riley, make furniture in her shop, and Wyatt bringing them dinner when they got so caught up in the work they forgot to eat. Homecoming dates and Ryder and Wyatt stealing a bottle of peach schnapps from one of the Gray Backs. The first time Wyatt held her hand, the first kiss. And the second kiss because he'd told her, "I can do better." And the first time they slept together...

Harper blew out a shaking breath and wrapped her arms around her stomach. Now he was different, and somehow even more enamoring to her than when they were kids.

With every hour she spent here, Wyatt felt more and more like her fire-starter, just waiting to ignite her.

"You shouldn't be out here alone," Wyatt murmured from the corner of the house.

Harper startled slightly, but offered him a smile. "There are three grown-ass shifters sleeping on the floor of your little house, and one of them is snoring like a freight train. I couldn't sleep. You?"

Wyatt shook his head and leaned against the logs of the cabin wall. He wore a pair of black, low-slung sweats, but no shirt. The blue moonlight illuminated his taut torso in alluring shadows and highlights, and his abs flexed with each shallow breath he took. With a sigh, he padded over to her and sat next to her on the top porch stair. "I needed to Change."

"And think. By yourself."

Wyatt smiled and rested his elbows on his knees, clasped his hands in front of him. "Yeah. I had a lot of thinking to do."

"You're used to being alone."

"That I am. I forgot how it was, you know? I forgot how everyone talks about everything, and calls everyone out on their shit. I got used to just me beating myself up." The corners of his eyes tightened as he stared at the full moon above the tree line. "Weston's right, you know."

"Wyatt—"

"No, just let me say this. I made so many mistakes with you. With myself. With everything. Growing up, my dad was always telling me how to be a good alpha and a good man, but somewhere along the way, I got so caught up in my own head I messed up. I veered off this easy path I had laid out for my future and went hiking in the damn brambles. And you...you paid for my mistakes." Wyatt arced that bright blue gaze to her, held her trapped there as he whispered, "I'm sorry, Harper. For all of it, I'm so sorry." He pulled a glossy, folded piece of paper out of his pocket and handed it to her.

With a frown, Harper unfolded it. When she realized what it was, she clasped her hand over her mouth to keep the heartache inside.

"I know you think I didn't think about Janey, or that I left you alone to deal with her loss." Wyatt pointed to the little ultrasound, to the tiny baby, no more than twelve weeks gestation, with little paddle hands and a round belly and knees tucked to her chest. "When you started bleeding, I had this awful, horrible thought that maybe if you lost her, it would be a good thing, because then you could live. I didn't really think you were losing her. I just had that thought. And when the doctors told me you were delivering, and that Janey was going to be stillborn, I couldn't go in there with you. I just paced outside the door. They said I needed to look at her for closure, but..." Wyatt scrubbed his hand down his face. "I couldn't go in there and look at our girl and watch your heartbreak, knowing I had wished that loss on us."

"You can't think it was your fault."

"I know it wasn't. I forgave myself. I was a stupid kid, just dealing with it the only way that made sense to me at the time, but this is what I have of her now. The cemetery, the hospital, that isn't my closure." He pointed to the ultrasound. "That is. That picture of my baby girl is my way of dealing with it."

Harper hugged the little picture to her chest and let off a long breath. "It feels like a million years ago now, doesn't it? Like another lifetime. So much has happened since then."

Wyatt nudged her arm, leaned over, and kissed the tip of her shoulder, then gave his attention to the moon again. "What did she look like?"

Harper traced the little baby and said, "She was a dragon."

"How do you know?"

"Two blue eyes, long pupils. Oh, she would've been a beasty like you. A strong girl. Maybe even a fire-breather like me. She was so *tiny*. Just..." Harper cupped her hands. "I held her in my palms, all wrapped up in a little pink blanket. "She was beautiful."

Wyatt wiped his cheek on his shoulder and wouldn't look at her anymore. But when she wrapped her arms around his waist, he hugged her against his side and let his lips linger on top of her head.

"Did you mean what you said earlier?" he asked in a hoarse voice.

"About wanting to bang in the parking lot of Drat's?"

Wyatt chuckled thickly and sniffed. "You know what I mean."

"I love you still, yes."

"As a friend or more?"

Her dragon let off a long, low growl in her chest. She didn't like giving too much for nothing.

Wyatt hugged her tighter against him and lowered his lips to her ear. "Because I love you, too. Always have. Always will."

He eased away just enough that his lips were inches away from hers. His gaze locked with Harper's, he froze and waited.

The choice was hers. Wyatt was giving her an out by hesitating, but she'd meant what she said in the truck. She loved him, and her soul had felt torn in two until she'd come here. Wyatt wasn't the boy who'd left all those years ago. He was different now. Mature. That much was clear from him taking Weston's blame in the truck and apologizing for all of it. He was a man who owned his mistakes, who wasn't too proud to say he was sorry.

He hadn't just left because he didn't love her. He'd left to punish himself, but it was enough that he was here, asking her to trust him and the man he'd become. Tonight, Wyatt had come out of that smoke ready to bring hell to earth and war to the supernaturals of Bryson City and Asheville to protect her.

And now this wild, quiet, loner of a man was admitting he loved her still? After all this time, he had pined for her, too?

Harper eased forward and pressed her lips to his.

Wyatt inhaled deeply, hugged her ribs tightly, and then pushed his tongue past the closed seam of her lips. He was fire in her stomach. He was the cool breeze and the scent of tree sap. He was everywhere and everything, filling her senses.

The only thing that was familiar about his kiss was his taste. Harper lifted the hem of her oversize night shirt as she straddled his lap, and Wyatt angled his face the other way, deepening their kiss.

Harper hesitated, her hands hovering just above his chest, but he pushed forward to meet them, and there he was. So warm and taut against her palms. His heartbeat was racing. She smiled into the kiss. Hers was racing, too.

Wyatt ran his hands under her shirt, over her panties, up her waist and ribs, and when he cupped her breasts, she moaned a helpless sound and leaned into him, encouraging his touch. A throaty growl rattled Wyatt's chest just under her palms, and gooseflesh raised over her arms at the sexy sound.

"Get a room!" Ryder called from inside. "I can hear you making out."

They did have a room, but Weston the professional cock-blocker was sleeping on the floor right beside Wyatt's bed.

Wyatt chuckled against her mouth and stood, taking her with him, straddled around his hips while he held the backs of her knees in place. So he could see where he was walking them, Harper lowered her lips to his neck and sucked gently. His growl was now steady, and louder. It wasn't the sound of anger, but the sound of satisfaction.

Wyatt's erection was hard against her soaking panties.

"Tell me you've sobered up."

"My dragon burned off the alcohol hours ago," she rushed out. "And I'm on birth control. Foolproof. A capsule in my arm keeps me safe for five years at a time."

Wyatt lengthened his stride and took her straight into the shadows of the tree line. He gathered her hair at the base of her neck and eased her head back as he leaned his shoulder blades against a tree.

He held her captivated for the span of three breaths before he snarled his lip back and clamped his teeth onto the healing skin of her neck, then released her, teasing her with a mark.

"Do it," she pleaded. They'd talked about him claiming her when they were teenagers, and she never thought she would get this second chance. "Please."

"Harper," Wyatt groaned, rocking his hips against her. He spun them and settled her on her feet, pressed her back against the tree. "We aren't there yet."

The pain in her middle at his rejection was instant. Slowly, she let her hands glide down his chest. Canting her head, she asked, "We aren't there, or you aren't there?"

Wyatt shook his head and looked off into the woods with an unfathomable expression. "A claiming mark is a big deal, and you're just getting to know me again. I want you to be sure when you ask for it next time."

He was still punishing himself then. Narrowing her eyes in a challenge, she leaned forward and bit down on his pec, just over his pounding heartbeat.

She clenched her jaw harder when he let off a helpless sound and bucked his hips. She wouldn't break his skin until he begged for it. And oh, she was going to get him to beg because she was good and done with waiting around for the man she wanted.

Hooking her fingers in the elastic band of his sweats, she pushed them down slowly, brushing her finger down the length of his swollen shaft as she went. It jumped and throbbed under her touch, and she couldn't help her smile. *Mine, mine, mine.*

Inside of her, the dragon that had been so unreachable earlier was drawn up, practically shooting off roman candles with excitement. After Harper pulled her touch from his shaft, he grunted, fell forward, and locked his arms against the tree as she dropped to her knees.

As she looked up and offered him a wicked grin, his eyes turned the color of ice. His chest was heaving, his arms flexed against the tree, abs so tight she could sleep in the damned trenches between each one. Slowly, teasing, she slid her hand down to his base and kissed the salty drop off the tip of his cock. Wyatt straightened and cupped the back of her head. He lifted his chin in that cocky masculine way of his she'd always loved. Guiding her, he pulled her closer and muttered a soft curse when she slid her lips over him. His hips jerked, and she knew she had him.

She taunted, because that was his real punishment for denying her. Harper took him slowly, then eased back. She ran her nails up his leg and cupped his balls on the next. Wyatt wasn't so patient now as he held her and thrusted into her mouth faster.

Faster and faster she took him until he jerked out of her mouth and released her head. Closing his eyes, he blew out three soft "Fucks," then pulled her up against the tree. "Don't want to come in your mouth. Not for our first time."

First time. They'd been together a dozen times when they were eighteen, but she understood. It hadn't been like this. They both had more experience now, and were different people. After all they'd been through, it was easy to appreciate the importance of his moment.

Wyatt's lips were all over hers, his tongue dipping rhythmically past her lips as he pressed his entire body onto her. Easing back by an inch, he pulled her shirt over her head and threw it onto the forest floor and, ooooh, she was melting. Melting into the tree, melting against his fiery skin, melting into this moment. She was so wet, her panties were soaking through. Wyatt leaned down and drew one of her nipples into his mouth until it tingled and drew up into a tight bud.

Arching her back against the tree, Harper looked up into the forest canopy above her and wondered how she'd gone so long without this. Without his mouth on her, without this feeling of completion. Wyatt dragged burning kisses up her chest and to her neck, allowing a hint of his teeth, and she was gone. He pushed his hand down the front of her panties and let off a long, feral sound when he slid his touch through the wetness he'd conjured between her legs. His breath hitching, he pushed his finger into her, gave her a few graceful strokes, then added another. She knew what he was doing. Wyatt was huge, and he was making sure she was ready for him.

Harper writhed against his hand. "I want more," she murmured. "I want you."

Riiiiiip. Her shredded panties were now in the dirt near her sleep-shirt, and Wyatt was shoving her knees farther apart. Here it was! The moment she'd dreamed of. The moment she'd imagined and touched herself to countless times.

Wyatt slid his shaft against her folds in a delicious tease. So close. Harper rolled her hips and caught his desperate kiss, gripped the back of his hair, and grazed her teeth against his bottom lip. Wyatt dipped into her by an inch, then lifted the back of her knee as he pulled back out. He eased into her slowly, stretching her, filling her. And he didn't stop until his hips met hers. "Wyatt," she whispered, disbelieving that anything could feel so good, so right.

Wyatt eased out and then pressed into her again, faster this time. And with every stroke, his abs flexed, hard as stone against her. And every time he hit her just right, she let off a needy noise that seemed to drive him mad and make him quicken his pace. Burying his face against her neck, he pulled her other leg around him and buried himself so deeply in her she gasped at the slight tinge of pain that mingled with the pleasure. He froze there for a moment, stayed deep, and thrust into her shallowly, hitting her clit with every smooth stroke.

Crying out with every thrust, clawing his back, she was lost to the intense pleasure he was building in her middle now. She felt everything so acutely. The tingling sensation in her center, the tree bark against her back, the rightness of their connected bodies, the rasp of his short facial scruff against her neck, the beautiful burn of his teeth grazing her healing throat.

"Come with me," he growled out as he slammed into her harder, but he didn't have to ask.

She was there. The moon was too bright now so she closed her eyes against the blue light and screamed out his name as orgasm exploded through her. Wyatt drove deeper, faster, and yelled out as his dick throbbed inside of her, shooting warmth into her core. He didn't slow, just bucked into her harder with every release of his seed until it was too much for her to hold. Warmth trickled down her thighs, and he froze, grunted with the final pulse of his shaft. Heaving breaths matching, Wyatt relaxed against her, held her tight. He brushed his lips against her neck and began moving slowing within her, drawing each aftershock out until her body was depleted.

She intertwined her fingers behind his head, and when she opened her eyes, she could see the old Wyatt there. The one who had loved her fiercely. Her eyes prickled with emotion, and she buried her face against his chest so he wouldn't see how affected she was. "I missed you so much," she said on a breath. "Don't ever leave me again."

Stroking her hair and hugging her tightly against him, Wyatt sighed and murmured, "My body left you, Harper, but my heart never did."

But it wasn't enough. She wanted his oath. She wanted a spoken promise from Wyatt because she saw so clearly the man he'd turned out to be. He was a man of his word. If he said it aloud, he would stick to it. She eased back and searched his blazing blue eyes. And then she whispered, "No leaving."

Wyatt smiled sadly and brushed a strand of hair from her cheek. "You'll be the one leaving this time."

Harper slid her arms around his neck, hugged him close, and stared into his woods over his shoulder. The woods his bear had claimed as his territory. The woods she didn't know. The woods that weren't home. He was here, in this new life he'd created for himself, and she didn't know where she fit into that.

My body left you…my heart never did.

Harper squeezed her eyes closed, and two tears ran down her cheeks.

She didn't know how everything got so messed up, but she knew one thing.

Her heart wasn't whole without him.

NINE

Clack...

Clack...

Clack...

Harper squinted her eyes open then moved the pillow she was hugging over her face to shield it from the sunlight streaming through the window. What were the boys doing this early? It didn't sound like chopping wood, but it had the same kind of echo.

Clack.

With a low rumble in her throat, she clicked her fire-starter once in agitation, then threw the covers off and rocked out of bed. One look in the mirror, and she yelped. She'd showered late last night after she and Wyatt had returned from their woodland boinking, and now she looked like she'd stuck a fork in a socket.

The noise continued as she brushed her teeth, straitened her hair, put on her make-up, and dressed. Curious, she kicked Weston's blankets out of the way of the door, then made her way out into the living room.

Aaron and Weston were sitting on the couch, just two grown men watching cartoons and eating straight out of the cereal boxes. Aaron tilted his head back and drank from the milk jug. Gross.

"Wyatt made you oatmeal an hour ago," Weston said without turning around. The cartoon was a trio of bouncing bears, dancing to a ridiculously annoying song about apricots and berries.

She moved to the table, peeked over the rim of the white ceramic bowl, and couldn't help the smile that stretched her face. He'd topped her oatmeal with honey, raisins, and cinnamon, just like she used to eat every day for breakfast her junior and senior year before Wyatt drove her to school.

He remembered.

Clack.

Harper grabbed the bowl and a spoon and meandered around the couch. Weston was wearing his favorite camouflage hat, and today Aaron had gelled back his longer blond hair. The crunching sound of their eating was constant as they took turns dumping cereal into their maws.

Aaron turned to another station, but it was just another cartoon. "God, the channels suck here," he muttered. And yet he kept watching.

Shaking her head, Harper made her way around the tossed blankets all over the floor where the boys had slept last night and onto the porch.

Clack.

The slap of a baseball against leather gloves was what she'd been hearing. Wyatt was playing catch with Ryder from an insane distance apart. The ball blurred through the air, barely visible it was so fast. Ryder caught it and hissed. "Damn, James, you haven't missed a step."

Wyatt had been the pitcher for their little league team when they were kids. Weston's dad and Wyatt's dad had coached the kids from Damon's mountains until they outgrew the sport. Harper sat down on the top porch stair since it was the only one not broken from the vampire attack that first night. Someone had hosed the vamp ashes from the porch, thank goodness.

She ate her cold oatmeal and smiled shyly when Wyatt gave her that sexy wink and crooked smile he used to be known for. Whew, he always drove the girls in the crews wild. He was the oldest—the chill, smart, confident one who had the biggest, baddest bear inside of him. He was destined to be alpha, like his father before him, and there had been something so sexy about barely harnessed power like that.

Harper had crushed on him for years before he wised up and held her hand at a homecoming dance.

"Remember when your dad and Mason took us on that road trip for that baseball game?" Ryder called across the clearing.

"Which one?"

"Montana."

Wyatt snorted and threw the ball back in a blur. *Clack.* "Yeah, Clinton went with us as a chaperone. He was supposed to help Dad and Mason wrangle us, but instead he gave us a bottle of whiskey, and we all got wasted on the hotel balcony the night before the game."

"Harper was the worst." Ryder nodded his chin to her and shook his head. "Sloppy then, sloppy now."

"Rude," she teased around a bite of breakfast.

"You did get us caught, though," Wyatt said, catching the ball. *Clack.*

"See, you all blamed me, but it was really Weston's fault. He was puking in the hotel bathroom half the night, and Mason busted him way before I admitted anything."

"Thanks a lot, Harper!" Weston called from inside.

"Wait, what?" Wyatt asked. "I didn't know that. Why did you let us give you so much shit over it?"

"Because I was a good friend," Harper said lightly.

"*Was,*" Weston called. "*Was* a good friend."

Mmm, mmm, mmm, Wyatt was a tall drink of water on a hot summer day. It was chilly this morning, and he was wearing one of those V-neck gray cotton shirts under a blue flannel he'd left unbuttoned. The color made his eyes look inhumanly bright. And with each throw, his movement emphasized his trim waist, long, powerful legs, and biceps bulging against the fabric. He sure grew up right.

"Dude, do you not work?" Ryder asked in a judgmental tone. "Is this your life? Just fighting vampires and sitting around at your cabin?"

Wyatt let off a single laugh. "Well, I was letting the Queen of the Asheville Coven drain my neck every few days for money, but now I'm out of that job."

"On account of you killing your employer?" Aaron asked from behind Harper.

Wyatt twitched his head as a dark look took his features. "Yes, sir. Other than that, I work at the gem mine hauling dirt for tourists and rock stores that sell it."

"Why would stores sell bags of dirt?" Weston asked from the open doorway.

"Because you never know. There could be a precious gem in there. Beryl and Corundum are guaranteed in every bag." Wyatt blasted the ball into Ryder's glove again. "The pay isn't great, but my bear needs it. I get to work heavy machinery—"

"An excavator?" Aaron asked.

Wyatt nodded and caught the ball. *Clack.* "Yeah, and I haul a lot of weight, which sates my bear. Kane works with me out there, and between the two of us, the owner doesn't have to employ a ton of labor. I asked for a couple days off, and my boss gave them to me. I've never taken any sick days before, and this week has been slow. The cold weather slows down tourist season."

"Sooo," Aaron drawled. "That's cool that Kane is your friend and all, but I saw his eyes after the fight last night when he didn't have his sunglasses on. Am I the only one freaked out by the fact that there is an unregistered dragon with fucking out-of-control lizard eyes in this town?"

Harper raised two fingers. "I'm bothered. He's a Blackwing."

"Whoa," Weston said. "Blackwing as in Marcus's line?" And now he was glaring at Wyatt again like Kane's existence was also his fault.

Wyatt threw the ball up in the air and then caught it easily with his glove. "Trust me when I say this—Kane isn't a threat."

"He beat me at arm wrestling," Harper argued. "And he eats peanuts out of the community bar bowl. Huge threat."

Wyatt's chuckle was interrupted by the ring of

his cell phone. "Oh crap," he murmured as he pulled his phone out of his back pocket. He frowned at the screen. "I have to take this. Harper, toss the ball with Ryder."

"Neeeeew," Ryder whined. "She throws like a girl." He looked at her scowl and muttered, "Just kidding, don't eat me."

Harper snorted. Her grandfather used to be a man-eater. She didn't enjoy the taste of people's ashes at all. Still, she'd threatened the boys within an inch of their everlovin' lives anytime they stepped out of line when they were kids.

Harper caught the glove and ball Wyatt tossed her, then watched him saunter off to the side, hand on his hip and back to them as he answered the call.

Ryder was eyeballs-deep in bullshit because Harper had been team captain of their little league team, a title she'd earned. She chucked the ball at him. He squealed and danced out of the way of her zinger, and at the last moment, reached to the side and caught it. Harper smirked when he rubbed his sore hand.

"Damn straight, I throw like a girl."

A few more rounds of that, and Wyatt hung up.

"Okay, so I want to show you all something."

"Hard pass," Weston said. "I'm about to leave."

"I really want you to stay, man. Just for a couple more hours. You've all asked me what I'm doing here, and I want to show you." Wyatt hooked his hands on his hips and gave Weston a pleading look. "Please. It would maybe explain some of the stuff you don't understand about me."

Weston slid his hat from his head, then replaced it with a pissed-off sigh. "Fine. Two hours, and then I'm out." He strode past Wyatt, hitting him in the shoulder with his own, and climbed up in his truck. "I'm driving."

Harper hugged Wyatt's waist and smiled up at him sympathetically. "You know Wes. His loyalty is hard to earn."

"I know. I broke his trust."

"So get it back," she murmured through a saucy grin. Feeling bold, Harper reached up on tiptoes and pressed her lips to his.

"Barf," Ryder called. "I'm barfing right now. I'm barfing in my mouth."

Wyatt laughed against her lips and angled his face, then thrust his tongue into her mouth once before he eased back with a sexy peck. Then he grabbed her ass hard and turned her toward the truck.

Damn that man could give her a serious case of the butterflies. Her stomach was doing gymnastics right now, and when she made her way to the pickup, she felt as drunk as she had all those years ago at that hotel in Montana.

"I call window!" Harper said, but the boys had already beat her to it. Aaron told her to "climb over" instead of moving his legs out of the way, the bunion.

"Where to?" Weston asked in a none-too-charitable voice.

"Take a right on the main road," Wyatt instructed.

"Town is left," Harper pointed out.

Wyatt shot her a quick grin and rolled down the window. "We aren't going to town."

He rested his arm on the edge of the door and relaxed back against the headrest. Now Harper had a perfect view of his gloriously chiseled jaw line. He'd shaved this morning, and he was somehow even more handsome under the scruff. And then, as if he could tell she was checking him out, he reached behind him and hooked his giant hand on the back of her calf and squeezed it once reassuringly.

Heat pooled in her stomach, and her cheeks blazed with pleased warmth. Ignoring Aaron and Ryder's eye rolls, she grabbed Wyatt's hand as he moved to pull away from her and kissed his palm quick.

Twenty-eight years old, and this man had her feeling like a teenager experiencing first love again. And maybe she was. Maybe this was normal for someone who had been through what she had. She was so infinitely relieved that he was back in her life and showing her the same affection, attention, and care that she felt for him. He wasn't holding back or treating her like she was temporary.

Instead, Wyatt was bonding them.

TEN

Aaron was angling his face down instead of looking out the window. He'd ridden like that for the twenty-minute drive into the Smokey Mountains. With a suspicious frown, Harper shoved his face to the side and gasped. His neck had been injured last night in the fight, but she hadn't even thought to check him this morning. Bear shifters had some of the fastest healing capabilities out of all the shifters, but Aaron's neck was only half-healed and angry looking.

Aaron lifted icy blue eyes to hers. A few strands of his gelled hair fell stiffly over his face. "It's not how I thought it would be with the vamps."

She studied the worry that pooled in his eyes. Aaron had always been the tough one. The quiet one. They'd spent summers and holidays together because their father's, Bruiser and Cody Keller, were half-brothers. She'd watched him grow up strong, and she'd watched him transition from a happy boy to a tattoo-covered, pierced, scruffy, motorcycle-riding badass. The changes started happening when he went through the Fire Academy to become a firefighter like his father and uncles. Something about his occupation had made him harder, more withdrawn.

She ran her finger over the injury on his throat. Hers looked much better than this, and the queen had her teeth on her longer. "Wyatt?"

Wyatt turned in the front seat, and his eyes dimmed. "Sorry, man. That shit'll scar. You went head-to-head with Aric, Arabella's Second. He wasn't trying to suck you dry. He was trying to rip your throat out."

Aaron twitched his neck out from under Harper's probing fingers. "Good. Chicks dig scars."

She hadn't missed the bitter edge to his voice. He didn't want comfort, though, and she'd learned from spending a lifetime around rough-and-tumble dominant shifters not to press him.

"Turn here," Wyatt said, pointing to a washed-out dirt road.

"Whoa," Harper murmured, leaning forward to look out the front window better.

The road was rough, sure, but there was no denying the beauty of these woods. It was early autumn, and the leaves were turning vibrant oranges, yellows, and bright reds. Sugar maple, sweetgum, scarlet oaks, and hickory trees lined the road in a myriad of sizes, and the ground was covered in the colorful leaves that had fallen early.

Up front, Weston tossed Wyatt a confused look she didn't understand, and Wyatt leaned out the open window and inhaled deeply. His shoulders relaxed on the exhale. Huh.

As they came to a rusty old gate with a lock on it, Wyatt murmured, "I got it." There were *No Trespassing* signs posted on either side that looked new, but the fence was old, and some of the posts had fallen over. Wyatt got out of the truck and jogged up to the gate, entered in a combination to the lock, then swung it open. He waited for Weston to pull through before he closed it and locked it up again.

"Uuuuh, I don't feel comfortable trespassing," Weston said, his dark brows jacked up high as Weston got back in the cab of his truck. "I'd like to not get shot by a landowner today."

Wyatt gestured out the window to a blue sedan that was parked on the side of the road up ahead. "The landowner knows we're coming. He was the one who called earlier."

Weston shook his head and bounced and bumped the truck up the road, spinning out in the muddy spots. An older man with glasses and thin hair on top of his shiny dome waved as they came to a stop. His smile was there, but it didn't reach his eyes. He looked...worried.

"Martin," Wyatt greeted him heartily, shaking his hand the second he was out of the truck.

"Hey, Wyatt. Thanks for coming on short notice. I thought for sure you'd be busy on your day off."

Wyatt introduced them to Martin one at a time as they piled out of Weston's ride. And when he got to Harper, Wyatt rested his hand on her lower back and said, "This is my...this is Harper."

Martin's bushy gray brows arched up

immediately. "Oh, wow." He gave two owl blinks and then shook Harper's hand vigorously. "I'm sure pleased to meet you."

"You, too," she murmured, baffled.

"Uuuh." Martin released her hand and gestured up the road. "I'll show you around."

Wyatt's eyes were boring into her, but she didn't understand the attention. Even as they walked up the muddy road and into a clearing, he kept casting her strange looks. It wasn't until she saw the cabin that she realized what was wrong with him.

He was watching her to see her reaction to the place.

The boys were dead-silent now, awed perhaps, or confused. She didn't know, but right now, she couldn't drag her gaze away from the old, dilapidated cabin to save her life.

The Smokey Mountain range painted the background like a picture, all oranges and yellows, and the woods were absolutely breathtaking. So different from the evergreen woods she'd grown up in.

Harper's breath came shallow as she made her way to the old cabin—a two-bedroom perhaps that had gone to disrepair. The porch sagged, and the railing was rotted. The roof was bad, and the picture window on the side was cracked in a couple of places. There was no paint on the log planks that made up the walls, and somehow, it felt like it was a part of these woods. Like it belonged, instead of sticking out like a manmade thumbprint.

There was a thin trail around craggy, tar-colored rocks that shone in the sun, and farther up the mountainside was another cabin. A double it looked like, from the twin doors and the breezeway that went right through the center.

Such an odd feeling came over her. A warm, prickling sensation that spread from her chest to her arms.

"What is this place?" she asked on a breath, so she wouldn't ruin the magic of this moment.

"Is it some kind of commune?" Ryder asked.

Martin chuckled. "No. My late wife's family has owned this land for generations. I run the gem mine, and when my wife was alive, this was where she dug in her heels. There are four cabins on the property. For twenty years, we rented them out to tourists for extra income, and my Betty managed the properties, but we got muscled out by a big fancy chain with new cabins, personal chefs, river views, hot tubs on every porch, the works. And when Betty passed, I couldn't keep up with the mine and manage the property, so…" He shrugged and shook his head. Resting his boot on one of the black rocks that jutted out from beside the path, he said, "I'm going to have to sell it. It's been draining my savings, and I'm wanting to retire soon. I've kept it for Betty, but we didn't have any children to give it to. I was hoping to find a buyer I know will take care of it.

Weston moved past her, eyes trained on something beside the door as he stepped carefully up the old porch stairs. With trembling fingers, he pulled up the last number of four that hung upside down from a single rusty nail.

Chills blasted across Harper's arms when she read the number. *1010*.

Wide-eyed, Weston looked back at Wyatt.

"I know," Wyatt murmured. "It's the same number as the old trailer up in Damon's mountains. I was never one for signs, but damn if that didn't draw me up when I saw it."

A shudder trembled up Harper's spine and

landed in her shoulders as she moved past Weston and pushed the door to the main cabin open. Inside, the place was dusty and made entirely of wood, from the floors to the walls to the kitchen cabinets and counters. There was a chair toppled over on its side and covered in cobwebs, and gingerly, she righted it and dusted off the seat. She could see the potential here. She could imagine polished floors and a small table in the corner with a vase and yellow flowers. Phantom laughter echoed through the house as she spun slowly, transforming it into a homey cabin in her imagination. Couches and pictures, and a TV stand over there.

The boys had filed in. "It's a shithole," Ryder said. "Needs a lot of work."

Wyatt's arms flexed as he crossed them over his chest. "Yep."

"It would cost you a lot of money to make the repairs," Aaron murmured.

"Yep." Wyatt's eyes were on Harper now, his gaze lightened, the scent of fur wafting from him. Why was he worked up?

"It's a drive from town," Ryder said as he ran his finger over the dusty window sill.

"Yep."

"It's right in the heart of vamp land," Weston murmured quietly from where he stood leaned against the front wall.

"That it is."

"It gets worse," Martin said from the open doorway.

"What do you mean?" Wyatt asked.

"I've been saving this place for you to come up with the money, you know that. But money is getting tight, and I still have bills at the mine to pay..."

"Okay," Wyatt said, a frown marring his face.

"Yesterday, I got a new offer."

Intensity sparked in Wyatt's blazing eyes as he stood up straighter. "Who?"

"The Valdoro Pack."

"Wolves?" Aaron asked. He shook his head and made a long *chhhh* sound.

"Shhit," Wyatt muttered. "Martin, trust me when I say you don't want wolves up here. You don't want them anywhere near here."

"I know that, Wyatt. But I've been holding onto this place for two years, and I'm getting to where I can't float it anymore."

"How much?"

"If you could just come up with what we talked about—"

"How much?"

Martin ducked his gaze to the dusty floor. "The alpha offered two hundred thousand."

Wyatt ran his hands through his hair and backed up a couple steps as though he'd been socked in the stomach.

"Can we talk in private?" Weston gritted out to Wyatt.

Martin offered them a sad smile and clapped his hand once on the open door frame. "I'll give you some time to absorb this. They gave me two weeks to decide. I just wanted you to know in case there's any way you can swing it." He made to leave but turned on the porch. "I'm sorry, Wyatt."

"What the hell is going on?" Weston asked, his gaze lingering on the old man who was sauntering to his car with a slight limp. "What is this place to you?"

"It's mine. My bear's. It feels like home and has since the moment I opened that gate for the first time." He pulled his phone from his back pocket. "Look." He showed them an image of a map of the country. There were red dots, yellow circles, and notes underneath. "I don't know if you're aware of the shortage of territory, but it's hard as hell for shifter to buy land now. The land has to be government approved to register a crew to it. But there is a grant program that will match a cash offer on approved land if it means a territory is settled by a good crew, pack, or coven. Twenty years ago, we didn't have territory problems because Vampires were still in hiding, and the wolves were, too. There were no rules, no laws about shifters owning big land, no financial assistance. Now, with the vamps and wolves out in the open, packs, covens, and crews are fighting for new territory."

"Yeah, I'm still stuck on the fact that we're in vamp territory," Ryder muttered.

"Everywhere is vamp territory!" Wyatt pointed to the yellow circles. There had to be a hundred of them, covering most of the country. "Damon's mountains were safe because of the dragon himself. But outside of them? It's hard finding a place to claim. I know because I've been searching for years."

"Then why didn't you just stay home?" Weston barked.

"Because Beaston said I was going to kill her!" Wyatt made like he was going to chuck his phone against the wall, but changed his mind at the last instant and snarled his lip. "I left because I thought I was saving Harper. Beaston told me I was going to be the death of her, and damn it all, I wanted her to live. She *had* to live. I wouldn't be okay if Harper didn't exist somewhere on this planet."

Harper backed away from the boys as the air thickened with the heaviness of dominance and riled up shifters. He'd left because he thought he was saving her? So it wasn't about him being a coward, or as aftermath of losing Janey.

"You think it was easy for me to tear myself away from her?" Wyatt yelled. His eyes roiled with blue fire, and his nostrils flared with fury. "Leaving felt like ripping my own guts out of my body and then going on with my life, pretending I wasn't some empty shell. And then I hear she has The Unrest. I heard it from Damon after her first seizure. He said it was my fault, and here I was suffering and hurting the woman I'd bonded to because I thought I was bartering my happiness for her life. So I went to work. I searched the entire damned country, every territory, desperate to stake a claim somewhere so that I would have something to offer her. To offer a crew because I knew it was too late for me to stop The Unrest alone. It's done. She's got it, and she already has the nosebleeds. This—" Wyatt jammed his finger out the front door to the autumn woods. "This was me trying to give Harper something so she'll be okay."

"Fuck," Aaron muttered, hooking his hands on his hips. He looked as gutted as Wyatt did right now.

Harper couldn't breathe. Wyatt had been working to claim territory, but not for his alpha-destined bear. For her.

Aaron flicked two fingers at Wyatt's scarred-up neck. "For money to buy this place?"

Wyatt huffed a humorless breath and nodded. "From that, saving every penny I've made at the mine, and working odd jobs, I've got fifty grand saved. I'm a hundred thousand shy still on the minimum Martin told me he would take for this place. The bigger the offer he gets from a crew, the more the government will match to have the territory settled, and this place is worth a lot."

"So what?" Weston asked. "You're going to set up

a territory here, you're going to recruit a crew and be the alpha your dad always swore you would be, and everything will just work out?"

"Weston," Ryder warned.

"No, I want to know the plan. I want to know why you didn't fucking tell us what you were doing! For years, you were just gone on your own. I hated you, Wyatt! I hated you for what you did to Harper. You let us all think you were a coward. You let us watch Harper wither, blaming you for every tear, every seizure. You couldn't fucking call us and explain what you were doing, *alpha*?"

"I don't want to be alpha."

"What?" Weston snarled, and now his eyes were black as pitch.

"Alpha should go to the most dominant shifter, yeah. But it should also go to the smartest. To the one who can keep a crew in line and who can stay objective in a fight. Alpha should go to someone who deserves it much more than me."

Ryder snorted. "Thank you. It's me, obviously."

"No." Aaron canted his head and narrowed his eyes at Wyatt. There was a faint smile in the slight curve of his lips. "Who?"

Wyatt dragged his blazing gaze to her and nodded his chin once. "Alpha should go to Harper."

ELEVEN

Well, Wyatt had laid it all out there, and from the silence at the table, it was clear as crystal the boys were out on this idea.

Weston hadn't said a word all through lunch and had a faraway look in his eyes, and Aaron and Ryder kept looking from Wyatt to Harper and back again with matching frowns.

Wyatt dropped a half-eaten french fry into his steak finger basket and leaned back. He hadn't tasted a single bite, and the silence was killing him. "Look, it's okay. It was my plan, and I missed it. It's not like I'm begging you to stay. I can't afford the territory anyway."

"I have ninety-three dollars in my savings account," Ryder murmured. "Even if I cashed out my retirement, it wouldn't be near enough. And I have a life! I have a good thing in Montana. No, it's not a lot of territory, but it's something. And I have a dog. I can't just pack up and move my whole life out here for land we can't even get."

"And you're talking about counter-offering against the Valdoro Pack, man," Aaron said softly. "Vamps are one thing, but you are going to put whatever crew pledges under you into a total free-for-all bloodbath. And it'll be you leading them, Wyatt. Look at Harper. She's had leaving in her eyes since the second you threw her name in the ring for alpha."

Indeed, Harper had been doing a really good job of avoiding his eyes since they'd left the property.

Harper ripped up the corner of a napkin. "It's just that I wouldn't make a good alpha—"

"Bullshit," Aaron and Ryder drawled out in unison.

"Yeah? And when I sicken? What happens to a crew under me then? We've all seen it through the years. A crew is only as good as its weakest link, and that would be me. The damn head of the crew would be the weakest."

Wyatt made a ticking sound behind his teeth in a soft argument. Harper didn't see in herself what he did. "You're a dragon—"

"A sick dragon, Wyatt. A sick one. Whenever one of the alphas has struggled over the years, what has happened to their crews? Huh?" She shoved her hamburger away with a disgusted look and raked her furious gaze from Ryder to Weston to Aaron to Wyatt. "Huh?" she asked again, louder.

"Chaos," Weston murmured.

"I don't want to go out like that. I don't want to be remembered for dragging you guys through hell with me."

Wyatt touched her leg gently. "You might not go out at all—"

"But I am! And I was okay with that. I'd accepted it, and now you're putting this beautiful offer in front of me and making me want more."

Wyatt slammed his hand on the table. "You should want more. You deserve it. You should be fighting."

Harper's dark hair fell in front of her face, hiding that gorgeous tear-rimmed dragon eye from him. "I should be fighting vampires and werewolves for territory I won't live through claiming? No, Wyatt. You should fight. Take out a loan, do what you have to do if the territory means that much to your bear. You were destined to be alpha, not me. Claim your land, recruit a crew...be *happy*."

"Harper—"

She shrugged and offered him a trembling smile. "It's what I want." And then she stood and dumped her uneaten hamburger and drink in the trash on the way out of the restaurant.

Outside the massive wall of windows, Harper hunched inward, and her dragon burst from her. Green, iridescent scales faded to gold along her belly. She wasn't as big as her grandfather, or even her mother, but she was beautiful. Spikes rose along her back like mountains, and two long ivory horns arched from the back of her head. Her eyes blazed blue, and as she opened her mouth to roar a deafening sound, she exposed a row of razor sharp teeth. She was breathtaking.

A couple of human women in the parking lot

were screaming in terror. Harper tossed one last look over her shoulder at the restaurant before she bunched her muscles and spread her wings. Leaping into the air, she caught the wind, and with powerful thrusts of her wings, she was airborne. Harper was grace in motion.

"She's leaving, man." There was a tinge of panic to Ryder's voice.

Wyatt blinked hard. He'd been so enamored with her Change he'd lost all logic. "What?"

"She's leaving!" Aaron shoved Weston's shoulder and bolted for the door. "Come on!"

"Shit," Wyatt gritted out as realization slammed into him. He sprinted out of the restaurant where the gravel grit was kicked up in a cloud from her take-off. "Harper!"

As if she could hear the ragged desperation in his voice, she beat her wings faster, lifting up and up, aiming for the thick cloud cover coming in from the south. No, no, no. Weston grabbed his arm and shoved him toward his truck as he passed. "Get in!"

Wyatt climbed into the passenger's seat, Aaron and Ryder in the back, and in a moment, Weston was peeling out of the parking lot, headed in the direction

Harper had taken off. The smell of Wyatt's own fur and the rubber from the skidding tires as Weston took a sharp left was suffocating.

"Do you have eyes on her?" Weston asked, squinting through the front window.

"She broke the clouds," Wyatt muttered, eyes on the dark shadow of her outline. *Dammit, Harper.*

"I lost her," Ryder said from where he was hanging out the back window.

Weston slammed his fist on the steering wheel and hit the gas even harder. "She's fucking running."

"I shouldn't have asked her—"

"Stop it," Aaron gritted out from the back seat.

"I shouldn't have! We were building something! I pushed too hard too fast. At least I had a part of her back. Fuuuck!" Wyatt yelled out the window, the curse tapering to a roar. He wouldn't be okay losing her now. Not after last night. He hadn't bitten her, no, because he wanted to take things slow for her. He wanted to be patient so he could keep her. But claiming mark or no, she was his. Always had been. And now she was bolting.

He deserved it.

Wyatt scrubbed his hand down his jaw. He

wasn't used to it without a beard, but he'd shaved for her because he didn't want to hurt Harper when they kissed. She was soft and perfect, and he'd been too rough against her last night. He'd stayed up, unable to sleep after they'd been together. He'd watched her for hours, watched the red rawness fade from her cheeks and swore he would hurt her less next time. He'd shaved because he thought they had more time together. *Stop thinking like that. You'll find her.*

"If you're going to Change, give me some warning," Weston ground out. "This is a new truck."

"I won't."

"You smell like a damn bear—"

"I won't! Just get us to the house. Maybe she went back there."

The boys didn't answer, though, and it curdled his stomach that they knew her better than he did. They'd stuck with her in her adult years. If they thought she was gone, she probably was.

Wyatt ground his teeth and held onto the oh-shit bar of the truck as Weston took a corner and nearly went up on two wheels. Gravel spewed behind them and *tink-tinked* against the metal bed.

Twenty minutes. It took twenty minutes to get

from the parking lot of Lottie's Burger Bonanza to his cabin, but it felt like an hour. Every second his heart pounded harder with the desperation to get to Harper. He would take it all back, all his plans. He could give her something simple. Date her until she was comfortable, and then someday a claiming mark. She didn't have to be alpha, or adhere to the pressure of this plan he'd set in motion. He'd fucked up and piled it on her too soon. She wasn't like she used to be. She wasn't the same girl who had practiced baseball until she outplayed the rest of them and earned captain. He'd been a fool to forget everything she'd been through that had shaped her into someone different. Into someone scared of letting the people she loved down. He got that. Wyatt had been a professional at letting people down.

Weston's truck went airborne over the last hill in front of his cabin, and he slammed on the brakes, skidding to a stop in the yard.

Harper's rental car was gone. "No," he murmured, stumbling from the cab of the truck. He searched the clearing, linked his hands behind his head and repeated his denial. "No." She didn't go. She couldn't have. Wouldn't have. She wasn't like him.

Harper was loyal and strong and didn't run out of fear. She'd proved that much when she'd gone after the vampires who were beating the shit out of him that first night.

She wouldn't leave without saying goodbye.

He sprinted for the cabin, threw open the door, and stumbled over the pallets the boys had slept on last night. His bedroom smelled strongly of Harper's dragon, smoke, the salt of tears, and her shampoo. But her luggage was gone.

Wyatt bolted for his closet and threw open the door, scanned it for her bag because he just couldn't believe it. Couldn't fathom her exiting her life like this.

With a feral snarl, he grabbed his truck keys from the hook by the front door and strode outside for his ride. The boys were standing around looking haunted, eyes tracking him as he passed, but let them think what they like. "I have to bring her back."

"Won't work, Wyatt," Weston murmured.

But fuck it all, he had to try.

It was an hour and a half to the airport, and if he gunned it and avoided the speed traps, maybe he could catch up to her and convince her their fates were intertwined now.

He would do anything. After the last couple days, he was ready to give up on his dream of claiming territory for his bear and go back to Saratoga if she would just let him in. He would happily face his past, and all the people he had bolted from, if she would just let him cling to her goodness. Because Harper was everything bright in his life, and he'd been too stubborn and scared to see that before. He was nothing without her. A ghost. A phantom. A zombie walking through life numb. Losing himself in the bottle and obsessing over territory didn't ease the ache anymore.

Only Harper did.

He would give anything in the world if she would just spend the rest of the time she had left with him.

TWELVE

Wyatt was exhausted by the time he got back to his cabin that night. It wasn't sleep he needed either, but emotional reprieve.

Weston, Ryder, and Aaron sat on the porch waiting for him, talking too low to reach his oversensitive ears as he pulled to a stop in the yard. As he approached slowly, none of them would meet his eyes, and their heads were tilted to the side. Probably best they not challenge his bear right now. All he wanted to do was Change and destroy everything.

"She didn't go to the airport, and she didn't turn

her rental car in. She's on the road somewhere, and I can't get a flight out to Saratoga until Wednesday." Wyatt ran his hands roughly over his head and stared at the night woods. Everything felt empty here now without Harper.

"It'll be okay, Wyatt," Weston murmured softly. His voice had that slight hitch of a lie though, as if he didn't really believe it.

Wyatt fought the urge to double over the pain in his stomach as his bear pulsed and clawed at him from the inside. "I've been working so hard and so long, trying to make myself worthy of her again, and now what? If I don't have her to fight for, what am I?" *Nothing.*

Ryder broke a twig into little splinters, and Aaron rested his head back on the porch railing, puffed air out of his cheeks as he stared out into the forest.

And Weston...he looked sick in the dim lighting. "I'm coming back for visits," he murmured.

It was then that Wyatt noticed a trio of dark-colored duffle bags near the boys on the porch. More pain in his middle. They were leaving. How was he supposed to go back to his lonely existence now?

Weston dragged his green eyes up to Wyatt and tried to smile. "And you'll visit Saratoga more because it'll be good for everyone. Spend whole weeks there. Linger at the holidays and go get sloshed with us down at Sammy's bar, and it'll be like you never left. You'll see."

"How do you know?"

Weston stood, shouldering his bag as he went. He came to a stop right in front of Wyatt, hesitated, then pulled him into a rough hug. Wyatt thought he would release him, but Weston held on tighter instead and gripped his shirt. "I just know." Two back cracking claps on his back, and Weston released him. He loaded up into his truck and drove away without looking back.

Ryder was next, but he didn't linger in his affection. Wyatt thought he was mad at him until he spoke.

"Call me. Please." His voice cracked on the last word, and when he eased away, Ryder looked gutted.

Shit. Wyatt looked up at the sky and begged the powers that be for strength as Ryder drove away. Today had started out the best day of his life and was ending one of the worst.

"She's the one for you, isn't she?" Aaron asked from right beside him.

Wyatt stared after Ryder's taillights as they disappeared into the woods. He inhaled deeply and blew out a long breath. "Yeah. I think she knew from when we were little. I figured it out at sixteen, and look what I did with it? I found the girl, Aaron, and then I waited until it was too late."

"Harper is loyal as hell. Always has been. It makes her an awesome friend, an awesome mate, but it also sets her up to get hurt. Give her time, but don't give up on her." Aaron clasped hands with him and pulled him into a hug. "It's damn good to see you, Wyatt. Damn good." With a sad smile, Aaron lifted his leg over the seat of his motorcycle and revved the engine. With a final two-fingered wave, he pulled out of Wyatt's yard and left him alone with the twinkling stars and the rustling leaves.

Wyatt winced at the pain in his chest and stumbled back into his cabin, determined to do what he used to do when Arabella would tear into his neck—drink himself stupid and stare at Harper's number. Fury boiled in his veins, not at Harper for running or at the boys for leaving. He was angry with himself. This should've gone different. If he hadn't been so stubborn all those years, he could have pulled this off. He should've had territory, a crew under him. He should've had a group of people he cared about under him, so that his bear could protect and provide for them like his instincts demanded.

In a flash of madness, he ripped the wooden board of key hooks off the wall and chucked it across the room. It splintered against the far wall and showered across the ground, and that's how he felt. Those ugly, jagged pieces were him, but for a day, he'd been glued back together thanks to Harper and the boys. What a sick feeling now to shatter again.

He snarled and pulled his phone from his back pocket, slammed his back against the wall, and slid down to the floor. And after a few minutes of desperate struggle to stay in his human skin, Wyatt called a number he hadn't touched in years.

"What's wrong," Weston's dad answered. He was Beaston, and when Wyatt had been a boy, he'd been terrified of the wild-eyed, barely under control Gray Back Crew mystic.

"Did you mean what you said all those years ago?" Wyatt asked in a hoarse voice.

"She won't die in childbirth. Not after what happened to Janey. She's strong like my Aviana. Like my raven boy. Like her mom and her grandfather and the Bloodrunners before her."

Beaston made no damned sense. He never had to Wyatt. Harper's female Bloodrunner ancestors had all died to bear young. They had to force themselves not to Change while they were pregnant to protect their offspring, and the females grew weaker and weaker until they bore their child. And then completely depleted, they passed within a few days of childbirth. "Am I going to be the death of Harper?"

No answer.

"Please," Wyatt whispered. "Am I?"

"That's up to you. Only you. Fate doesn't know what to do with two alphas anymore. One dragon, one bear—apart they are broken, but whole together. You messed with the Bloodrunner Dragon's destiny." Beaston swallowed audibly over the line. "She went home, boy."

"I've already booked a ticket to Saratoga—"

"This ain't home. The Dragon went somewhere that *feels* like home."

The phone went dead, and Wyatt frowned at the

darkening screen.

And slowly, a tiny tendril of hope unfurled inside of him, easing the burn of the bone-deep ache in his chest.

THIRTEEN

Alpha. Wyatt had lost his damned mind.

Harper shook her head for the hundredth time since he'd aimed that ridiculous word at her. Dragons weren't alphas. They thrived alone, bonded to one mate, and females like her died off young. Other than the dragon wars in ancient times, that little genetic anomaly was the biggest reason for the near extinction of her kind.

Bears, wolves, big cats, and other apex predators made good alphas for crews, but only if they were dominant and healthy, both physically and mentally. She was none of those things.

Harper snapped the lock on the gate and tossed the mangled metal to the side, then pulled the wadded-up shirt back to her bleeding nose.

She'd tried to leave, really she had, but she'd been thirty minutes outside of Bryson City when the biggest, longest seizure of her life had taken her. She'd nearly died on the side of the road, unable to escape her seatbelt, trying desperately to keep her foot on the brake so she wouldn't go careening off the old bridge in front of her and into the river. And when she'd recovered enough to drive again, her dragon had balked and wouldn't let her take her foot off the brake until she threw the car in reverse.

Okay then, she wasn't headed for the airport tonight, but with a little luck, she would feel better tomorrow morning and start making her way back to Saratoga. So she could die alone.

She grimaced and shoved the gate open. No, not alone. She had the boys. They would visit like they always did, and call her. Her cell phone lit up with a message, asking for a video chat. Wyatt's number flashed on the screen. Nope. She rejected the request and shoved the phone into her back pocket. She wasn't ready to make apologies or have him see how badly her nose was bleeding. She just wanted one night to mull over everything that had happened today without Wyatt or the boys in her head. And Martin's vacant property was the best place to do that.

She drove through the open gate, left it swung wide, and made her way down the muddy road to the clearing where cabin 1010 sat.

The problem lay in the moments following Wyatt's declaration she should be alpha. It was the look of a lightbulb going off over Ryder's head, the slow grin on Aaron's lips, and the baffled there-it-is expression on Weston's face. It was the hope in Wyatt's eyes.

She was going to fail them. The last thing she wanted on this earth was to throw them into chaos before The Unrest took her. And it wasn't a crew of strangers who had been recruited either. It was the people she loved the most, her best friends, the ones who had kept her propped up with their strength when The Unrest began. She couldn't do that to them.

Harper got out of her car and pulled her bag from the back seat, then made her way up to the dark cabin.

It should be creepy, being in these unfamiliar woods so late at night and in the pitch darkness, but such a feeling of safety washed over her skin that she paused right before the porch steps and closed her eyes, breathed in the crisp mountain air. It smelled different here than back home. Home. Was Saratoga home? Now she didn't know. Her feelings were mixed, and she frowned as she realized home wasn't really a place for her anymore. It was Wyatt. Maybe it had been him all along, and that's why things had gotten so messed up. Her dragon chose a lair that didn't stay in one place. A lair with the ability to leave, while she stayed stagnant and pining for something she couldn't force to be hers.

A sigh of relief expelled from her lungs as she stepped into the cabin and turned on the light. The dusty old house was her sanctuary tonight, and when she drew the shirt away from her nose and pressed her fingertip there, she was baffled to find it had suddenly stopped bleeding. Maybe it was coincidence. It had been going for half an hour now and had to stop at some point. It was probably the applied pressure that had staunched it.

There wasn't anywhere clean to sit down, much

less sleep, so Harper dropped her bag and the bloody rag and made her way into the small kitchen. One peek under the sink, and her face was consumed with an unexpected smile. Martin's late wife must've been a thorough cleaner because it was chock full of supplies. And in the closet was a good broom and dustpan.

So as Harper's mind swirled round and round all that had happened over the last couple of days, she worked. Dragons were tidy by nature, and she had always relieved stress by cleaning. This was different, though. With every sweep of her broom, she adored the rich color of the floorboards a little more. With every wipe of the rag over the countertop, she admired the craftsmanship and smoothness. She even memorized the little cuts in the natural sealed wood where people had dinged the surface over the years. With every scrubbing motion in the sink, she admired the shine. Hours passed like minutes. And when she dumped the final dustpan of dirt off the front porch and turned to the open doorway of 1010, with its warm glow spilling over the sagging but swept front porch, such a strange sensation buzzed through her chest. At first, she feared it was another seizure come to take her too soon, but as the seconds ticked by and she didn't double over in pain, she pressed her open palm gently over her chest.

It wasn't the humming of The Unrest. It was a content sound her dragon hadn't made since she was a child. It was a sound she'd assumed she had outgrown.

The porch floor boards groaned under her feet, and behind her, the crickets chirped. The breeze made rustling music with the creaking tree branches. She couldn't take her eyes off the polished wood floors through the open doorway. 1010 was beautiful, despite the cracks in the windows and the age of the cabin.

Stunned, Harper took a step backward and rested her hips against the porch railing. Crossing her arms over her chest, she canted her head and squinted at the doorframe thoughtfully. She'd been living in Pop-Pop's cliff mansion in a room dug deep into the cave walls. She'd slept to the *drip-drip* of water falling from the stone wall behind her bed and thrived with the dank, cool air against her skin. Her room at her grandfather's house had been built for dragons like her, so why was this place singing to her? It was the opposite of what she was supposed to covet. Why was this old, hole-infested cabin drawing the constant, happy vibration from her inner dragon?

The sound of Wyatt's truck engine sounded up the road, and Harper's lips curved in a smile that felt good. He'd found her. Of course, he had. They were bound by their souls, by their destinies. Of course, he would know her heart.

Three hours ago, she would've been prepared to tell him she needed space and time, but now she didn't want to experience this happy, elated moment alone. She wanted to spend it with him.

The sound of the door shut, but Harper was too afraid to turn around in case the happy noise ceased in her chest.

"I'm sorry," Wyatt murmured from behind her.

At the tone of his voice, the sound in her chest rattled louder. "Come here," she whispered as tears prickled her eyes.

The *creak creak* of the porch stairs sounded, and then he was there. Her Wyatt. He was tall and strong, and his eyes churned with intensity as he searched her face. He lifted his fingertips to her cheek and then stroked a strand of hair, tucked it behind her ear.

"Are you okay?"

She laughed thickly and pulled his hand to her chest, pressed it over her heart.

He froze, his eyebrows lifted, his lips slightly parted. They stood like that for the span of three heartbeats, connected by that simple touch. And then Wyatt whispered, "I remember this. I lived for this sound once."

Harper bit her trembling lip and admitted, "I never thought I would hear it again."

When Wyatt dragged her against his hard torso, his body melted against hers like a second skin. He swayed them gently from side to side and then lowered his lips to her ear. "I don't want you to run. I want you to stay here and fight. I want you to spend every minute you can with me. Not because I deserve the second chance, but because I love you so much I can't imagine being apart again. Forget what I said about alpha. I know I put pressure on you in front of everyone, and I'm sorry. You don't have to be anything other than who you are, right now. It's more than enough for me."

A sob wrenched up her throat, and she clung to him tighter. "I wasn't scared before, but then I came here and felt so deeply again because of you. And now I want more time. I'm afraid I won't find my place before the end."

"Your place is with me, here or in Saratoga or wherever makes you happiest. I'll be there for you. And no more talk of the end."

"Wyatt—"

He eased back and cupped her cheeks gently. His eyes were full of promise as he murmured, "If I have one day with you, or twenty, or a year...we won't waste another moment running. Not a single moment, okay? I'm yours. I've always been yours."

A soft, shuddering whimper of relief was all she was able to manage before he kissed her. This moment, this instant, eclipsed all others. Standing here in the warm glow of 1010, she melted against the man who held her heart. Who had always held her heart.

Forget what they'd gone through to get to this moment. It had all been worth it to feel the depth of this happiness. Of this joy. Wyatt brushed his tongue against the closed seam of her lips, and she parted for him with a relaxed sigh. Too soon, Wyatt eased back and rested his forehead against hers.

"Harper?"

"Yeah?"

"Do you want to stay here tonight?"

With a mushy smile, she nodded.

"Okay, wait right here. I brought you something." Wyatt grinned and then jogged off the porch to the back of his truck. And then he reappeared lugging a queen-size mattress like it weighed nothing.

A shocked laugh bubbled up her throat as he maneuvered it into the cabin. "How did you know I would be here?"

Wyatt let the mattress fall onto the floor. "Beaston told me. Kind of."

With a squeak, she ran, then spun in the air and landed on the soft cushion of the mattress and stared up at the rafters with a grin plastered to her lips. Wyatt disappeared outside again and then returned with a pair of pillows and an armload of the blankets from his bed.

"Remember the first time we snuck out to that tree house we used to all play in?" Harper asked him. God, she hoped he remembered because it was one of her brightest memories. It had been the day everything changed for them. It was the day she'd wiggled her way out of the friend zone.

He chuckled as he straightened the covers over her. "How could I forget. You stuck your hand down the front of my pants up there." He flipped off the light switch. "I don't think I've ever been more shocked," he said in the dark, amid the rustle of fabric.

"Okay, but I'd liked you for years, and I had been holding back for so long, thinking about you, wishing you would kiss me, wishing you would touch me and just give me a clue that you liked me back as more than a friend. I saw you flirting at lunch with a couple of human girls the day before, and I just knew I had to make my move."

"You could've said, 'Wyatt, I like you,' at any time." He let off a laugh and flopped down on the bed next to her. "I take that back. The way you told me was perfect. I'd always thought you were pretty, but I just never thought I had a chance with you." He rested his arm under her head and drew her close, kissed her forehead. "You were this tough, mature dragon-girl. You were always out of my league, so I didn't even think about going after you until you let me know I had a shot."

"Coward," she teased, nuzzling her cheek against his chest.

"Hell, yeah. You had the fire, Harper. Everyone was a coward around you."

She giggled and traced his puckered nipple. He'd taken his shirt off, and his skin was so warm. She'd always run hot, but Wyatt almost matched her heat—more proof he was her match. Her skin didn't burn him. He was strong enough for her.

His voice dipped low and serious. "That night in the tree house, I knew I was done for. I remember walking you back home before dawn, and we'd just kissed for the first time. You'd touched me, and I couldn't leave you."

"What do you mean?"

"I mean...I sat under your window until it was time to get up for school because my bear wouldn't let me leave you."

She frowned and rested her chin on his chest, stared at him to make sure he wasn't teasing. "You only lived a few trailers away from me."

He huffed a quiet breath. "It was still too far, Harper. After that, I *lived* for when you asked me to meet you at the treehouse because it meant I would get to hold you and feel okay without the guys giving me shit, or your parents giving me those worried looks because we were so young to be forming a bond, you know?"

"Yeah," she murmured as flashes of memories ran through her mind. She had so many good ones that involved Wyatt. "Do you remember when my dad caught us sneaking back into my trailer when we were seventeen?"

"Oh, God," he said in that sexy, deep timbre of his. "Bruiser was terrifying, and your mom is a freaking dragon shifter. Then I had your birth mom lecturing me, and Drew threatened to maul me. You weren't an easy girl to date, you know. I thought Bruiser was gonna pummel me when we got busted, but I understood. He was just lookin' out for you."

"He took you out in the woods the next morning..."

"Yeah for the most uncomfortable sex talk ever. It included death threats. And when I got home, my dad gave me the same one and begged me to leave you alone. Your dad's bear was on a tear for a while after that, and my dad was trying to be an understanding alpha."

"Keeping us apart didn't work, though. I loved you too much by then. My dragon had already picked you."

In the soft glow of the moonlight streaming through the cracked window, the vacant smile faded from Wyatt's lips. "And my bear had chosen you."

"Swear you'll never leave me again, and I'll believe you," she whispered. "Swear it, and I'll never question it again."

"How, Harper?" He shook his head and cast his attention to the rafters above them. "How could you not question it all the time, even if I swore?"

"Because you're a man now, Wyatt. You aren't that flighty boy you used to be anymore. You've changed in good ways. Swear it."

Wyatt's chiseled jaw clenched, and he turned his face on the pillow, locked his gaze with hers. "I swear on my life I'll never leave you again, Harper."

"Good," she said on a breath. Her heart pounded in her chest as she lifted off him slightly and kissed his pec. When she sucked hard just over his heart, a soft groan came from deep in Wyatt's throat. He cupped the back of her head, drew her closer, encouraging her. This was it. This was the moment she'd waited her whole life for. Her breath trembled as she grazed her teeth over his skin. Wyatt's hips rocked, and he angled himself toward her, pulled her body against his.

Leaning forward, he drew her sensitive earlobe between his teeth, then whispered, "Do it."

This would change everything. It would complete their bond, and her dragon would no longer be able to be away from him. He would be as vital to her as air. And as terrifying as it was to trust someone so completely with that power, it was Wyatt. Her Wyatt.

She drew her fingernails up his back and sucked again on his chest, teasing until his erection was hard against her belly. Clenching her jaw, she pierced his skin with her teeth, bit down harder and harder as he gripped the back of her head. The taste of iron coated her tongue, and Wyatt rattled off a long snarl as she bit hard enough to scar, then released his torn skin.

The humming sound was back in her chest, but the adrenaline that had dumped into her veins was making her tremble with the gravity of this moment. She'd never in a million years thought she would get a second chance at this, and here he was, pledging himself to the remainder of her life. Wyatt dipped down and sucked the taste of pennies from her lips. This kiss wasn't soft or gentle, but was the affection of a man on the edge of his control.

He thrust his tongue inside her mouth over and over and angled his face the other way as he rolled on top of her. With a snarl, she yanked her shirt over her head in one smooth motion and broke the front clasp of her bra and oh, my, damn, Wyatt was setting her on fire right now. Her body ached for him, and her breasts tingled with anticipation as he worked his biting kisses down her throat and chest. He drew the bud of her nipple between his teeth, too rough and not rough enough. She hissed and arched her back against the mattress. Wyatt let off a feral sound and threw the covers off their legs and onto the floor, then he unsnapped her jeans and rucked them down her legs to join the pile. His lips were hot against her belly, and then his teeth were on her hipbone, teasing her. God, she wanted him. Gripping his hair, she spread her legs wide and guided him into the cradle she'd created. They'd never done this before, but right now her belly was on fire for him to kiss her there.

And then his mouth was on her, his tongue brushing up her clit, sucking, laving. The moonlight was too bright, but she couldn't stop watching his head bob between her legs. Clever man, bringing her closer to climax with every lick. But she wanted more.

"Wyatt, please," she begged shamelessly.

His growl rattled against her sex, and then she felt it. He drove his tongue deep inside of her, and she cried out, tossed her head back against the pillow. His hands gripped the tops of her thighs hard, causing pleasure and pain. She was utterly lost to the waves of sensation that rocked her body. Another thrust of his tongue, and then another. She gasped. "I'm gonna come," she whispered, warning him, but it only seemed to spur him on. He sucked her clit and then drove back inside her until orgasm exploded through her.

Harper's body shuddered as he encouraged every aftershock with that sexy mouth of his. And oh, his bear was a snarly monster right now, like he couldn't get enough of her taste. She felt like a goddess as she twitched and writhed against him.

Wyatt eased back, sucked on her inner thigh, and

then chuckled a warm, sexy sound as a tremor took her body. "One," he murmured.

Holy hell, her man wasn't through.

Wyatt sat up, legs folded under him, thick erection jutting out between his legs, the epitome of a rutting, mature male. With a wicked grin, he trapped her in his blazing blue gaze and gripped the base of his dick, ran a slow stroke up to the tip, and then pushed into his hand again, his powerful abs flexing with the smooth motion. He blinked languidly and lowered his attention between her legs. Feeling reckless, Harper spread her knees wider and tossed him a challenging look. She clicked her fire-starter once and jerked her chin. *Come here. Please me.*

Wyatt's sensual lips curved up in the corners as he crawled over her. On hands and knees, he lowered his lips to hers as she ran her hands up his bulging triceps. He spread his knees wider, lowering himself down against her thighs, and with a graceful roll of his hips, his cock pushed inside of her by an inch. He let off a deep huff of breath and eased out, then pressed back in. So big. *Relax so you can take all of him.*

Harper traced the bite mark that had streamed

crimson down his chest—her declaration that she was his always. He clamped his teeth on her hand teasingly, then pushed into her deeper. She gasped with how right he felt filling her up like this. "Deeper," she demanded on a breath.

Wyatt's eyes lightened to a snowy color as he slammed into her hard. He eased back slowly, then flexed his hips hard again. He lowered himself onto her until there was no end to her body, no beginning to his. Burying his face against her neck, he bucked into her harder and faster, his snarl matching the humming vibration in her chest. His abs flexed hard against her stomach with every thrust. The pressure was growing too fast, too bright. She cried out with every stroke, and now his hands were gripping desperately hard to her back and waist. His teeth grazed her shoulder, right above her collarbone, and potent desire washed through her.

Please, please, please.

He slammed into her harder, their bodies making a slick sound as they drove each other closer to climax. Teeth, teeth, teeth. So sharp. Right there. *Do it!*

Harper screamed out his name as she came hard.

He froze inside of her and bit deeply into her skin as his dick swelled and pulsed the first jet of wet heat into her. Mindlessly, she chanted his name over and over as he bit down harder and thrust into her again. She was clutching onto him so tight now, desperate for him to bite her deep enough to count. Desperate for every body-shattering pulse of pleasure he conjured between her legs.

Wyatt grunted and released her skin, then slammed into her again as his dick throbbed on, matching her orgasm. "I love you, Harper," he murmured in a voice that was gravel and velvet. "I love you so much."

Her shoulder hurt badly, but she'd never been happier in her life than in this moment. "I love you, too," she whispered through her tightening vocal cords. She cupped his cheeks and looked up into those beautiful inhuman eyes of his. "I've waited so long..."

"I know. Me, too." Wyatt relaxed on top of her and cupped the back of her head gently as he lowered his lips to hers. He sipped at her until every last pulsing aftershock had faded. And when she was sated and utterly stunned by what had just happened, she kissed the bite mark on his chest. "You're mine now."

His smile was so genuinely happy, it rendered her breathless. Wyatt rolled over, taking her with him, and hugged her so tightly against him she could barely draw a breath. His cheek against hers, she could feel his smile there as he told her, "I always was."

FOURTEEN

Wyatt hit the lever to lower the bucket and scooped another layer of earth from the mountain. The excavator jumped and twitched under him as he hit a layer of rock, but he adjusted and pulled up, then drew it over the back of the dump truck and emptied the mine dirt on top of the pile.

"Full enough," Kane called. "Shut her off."

Wyatt cut the engine and hopped down the side of the giant machine, eager to get this work day done so he could go back to his mate. Wow. Wyatt huffed a soft laugh. *His mate.* How had he gotten so damn lucky?

Kane was glaring at him through narrowed eyes, and that shit always freaked him out. Kane had those green snake eyes that didn't belong in a man's face. He usually wore sunglasses to cover them up in public, but when he was about to ream Wyatt, he always left them off. Intimidation tactics, but it wouldn't work on him. Not today. He was too high up on cloud nine.

Wyatt grinned brightly and sauntered past him, then climbed into the passenger's seat of the dump truck.

"What's going on with you?" Kane asked as he limped to the driver's side and pulled himself up. He had a bum leg, but every time Wyatt asked about it, Kane shut him down and wouldn't talk to him for a week, so okay. They weren't crew, and they weren't friends. They were tentative allies since the vamps posed a threat to both of them.

"I don't know what you mean," Wyatt said through a baiting grin.

"You've been smiling all fucking morning. And your bear feels different. And furthermore, you've become quite the popular man in town right now."

Wyatt rolled down the window as Kane circled

the dump truck toward the old mining road that led down toward the tourist section of this gig. "What do you mean?"

"I mean Aric and a few of his vamps have been hanging around the parking lot of Drat's at night. Last night he finally came in and asked about you right-out. The only thing keeping them from going after you at your place is the Bloodrunner Dragon."

"She has a name."

"Fuck her name, Wyatt. If she leaves, your jugular is wide open for the ripping."

"She ain't leavin'."

"Everyone leaves, man."

"I did Aric a favor. He's king now. He should be shaking my hand and buying me a shot."

"It doesn't work like that, and you know it. Look, I know we don't see eye to eye on stuff, but if you go down, I'm next. And I like it here. I'm sick of moving around."

"Then pick a damned territory, Kane. You're a Blackwing Dragon, man. You don't need anyone's protection."

He made a pissed-off clicking sound behind his teeth. "You know it's not like that for me. I don't need a treasure like the Bloodrunner."

"*Harper*. Her name is *Harper*." Wyatt pulled the hem of his T-shirt up until he exposed the puckered, angry-looking claiming mark on his pec. "She's with me now. Fighting another dragon in your territory won't work. She isn't your enemy. She's good."

Kane looked over at his mark with those blazing green eyes, back to the steep road, and then back to him before he murmured, "That's a really big deal."

"Yeah." Wyatt straightened the thin fabric of his shirt back in place and took off his hard hat, tossed it to the dusty floorboard between his work boots. "It feels like I've been waiting my whole life for this. If Aric wants trouble, he's barking up the wrong tree. Now that Harper knows alcohol inhibits her dragon, she won't make the same mistake twice."

"Would you die to keep her safe?" Kane asked so quietly Wyatt almost didn't hear him over the roar of the engine.

"Yeah." It was the easiest answer in the world.

Kane sighed, and his breath tapered into a growl. "Look, Aric isn't the only one asking about you."

Wyatt frowned at Kane's profile. "Who else?"

"The alpha of the Valdoro Pack came in last

night, too. Axton something-or-other. He and his wolves are in town to put pressure on Martin to sell faster, and he isn't a fan of yours. He told me to tell you he wants you out of the territory the second the deal closes."

Wyatt groaned and pressed the heels of his palms against his eyes to ease the tension headache building there. "Fuckin' wolves, man. I miss when the vamps and wolves were still in hiding. At least they policed themselves better then. Now the leaders have too much power and zero moral compass."

"You're preaching to the choir. Wolves will ruin this entire town. It won't be safe for families anymore, and tourism will grind to a stop. They'll bring bloodshed to the Smokies." Kane cast him a quick, thoughtful glance. "Look, I only picked up the shifts at Drat's for extra income. I have some money saved."

"For what?"

Kane turned onto the backroad that led down to the tourist center of the mine. "I have ten grand I can put up for the territory, no strings attached."

"What? Why? You barely tolerate me."

"It's not for you, dumbass. I have my own

interest in mind. I can't defend a territory on my own, but between you, your Bloodrunner, and any crew you recruit, you could. If you don't set up territory here, I'm out. I have to go on the run again, and I'm so fucking tired of running."

Wyatt scratched the back of his head in irritation. "It's still not enough. Not by a lot. We'd still be about ninety thousand short, and really, I should be matching the Valdoro Pack's offer because they'll kill Martin if he shows favoritism."

"How short are we if we match their offer?"

"One-forty."

Kane shook his head for a long time and smelled pissed off, but there was nothing to be done about that. Wyatt had quit beating himself up over the things he couldn't control. Chronic guilt was a slow poison his bear had buckled under, and Wyatt liked to think he'd learned his lesson.

Emotionally crippling his bear with remorse wasn't a viable option anymore.

Harper was enduring The Unrest, and would need him to be whole and strong for her.

FIFTEEN

Harper licked her bottom lip in anticipation and stepped onto the rickety bridge. The uncomfortable humming of The Unrest buzzed just under her skin, so she stepped back.

It couldn't be.

She tried again, and this time, her nose tingled with the smell of iron, and deep within her, the dragon let off its warning rumble.

"Mother trucker," she whispered as a smile stretched slowly across her face. Gooseflesh rippled up her arm and landed in the claiming mark Wyatt had given her last night. The torn skin was half healed, but it ran hotter than the rest of her as a constant reminder that she wasn't alone. That she wouldn't be alone ever again because he'd bonded them completely.

And now this?

When Harper stepped onto the bridge again, her dragon snarled, and the first drop of warmth trickled down onto her lip. In a rush, she backed up and ran her hand under her nose. Just one drop, and it was done. She wanted to laugh and scream and cry and laugh some more because never in her life had she thought her dragon would do this.

She couldn't leave. She didn't want to. Nothing in her wanted to take her rental car to the airport and fly back to Saratoga. Every instinct she possessed screamed that if she was going to be okay, it would have to happen here, in a little town near the Smoky Mountains.

Rubbing her arms to put warmth back into them, she jogged for her car and yanked her phone from her purse with trembling hands. She had to try twice to scroll to the right contact. Sebastian Kane had handled her investments and retirement for the past decade. She had savings, but she needed more if she was going to do what her dragon had been roaring for her to accomplish since last night.

"We was just talkin' about you," Bash greeted her.

She giggled and asked, "Oh yeah? Are you over at Asheland Mobile Park today?"

"Nah, your dad came to see me. We're drinkin' beer up at Bear Trap Falls. Too bad you ain't here. I bought that fruity shit for you and my girls. I didn't even know you'd left the mountains until Bruiser told me a minute ago."

Harper's smile dipped slightly. Bash's three daughters must be home visiting, and she was missing seeing them. If she couldn't leave here, she would always miss what was happening back in Saratoga. Holidays, birthday celebrations, Lumberjack Wars, all of it.

Was this what it was like for Pop-Pop? Was he stuck in his mountains for always?

The sound went all muffled, and static blasted across the line like fabric rubbing against the speaker. Bash said, "Hey Bruiser Bear, your daughter called me before she called you, ha ha!"

"She called me and Diem yesterday, you dipshit."

Yep, that was Dad.

Harper snickered and said, "Hey Bash Bear, I need to pull some of my money."

"She wants money," Bash said in that muffled voice.

Dangit, she didn't want to do this with Dad right there. She'd planned on telling him and the rest of the crew if this actually worked out.

More static, and Dad asked too loud into the line, "You in trouble?"

"No. I swear I'm not. I'm..." Well, here it goes. "Dad, I think my dragon picked a treasure."

"What?" There were a few beats of silence then louder, "What? Baby, don't you be teasin' me." God, there it was, that tremor that said Dad was getting choked up. "W-what is it?" He was yelling. "Dammit, Harper, talk! What did she pick?"

Harper clapped her hand over her mouth at how relieved and hopeful Dad sounded. "She picked Wyatt. And I think some land in North Carolina. Mountains. Up in the Smokies. I'll need all of my savings and most of my investments in order to make a fair offer."

"Oh my God, oh my God, oh my God. I have to tell

your mom and Riley. Drew is gonna shit himself. Baby, are you sure? Wait...Wyatt? You found him?"

"I found him, Dad." She swallowed a sob and blew out a steadying breath before she whispered, "He claimed me."

Dad was quiet so long she thought he'd maybe hung up on accident. But then her father, big old burly Bruiser Bear, sniffed, and that tiny noise told her he was crying for maybe the first time she'd ever known about. "We've been waiting a long time for that boy to come around." Dad's voice came out hoarse and thick.

"He's not a boy anymore. He's really different. He has a dominant grizzly, but he has him controlled. Has him steady. Has him wanting a crew under him. He's been saving up money to buy territory."

"For his crew?"

"No. For me. So he could save me."

Dad's sigh shook like a leaf in a stiff wind. "I'll give you back to Bash so you can talk money, but Harper?"

"Yeah, Dad?"

"You did it."

"What do you mean?"

"I know you always hated that your dragon hung onto people too hard, but your mom and Pop-Pop are the same way. It's just how you dragons are. You lock your heart onto someone, and then you never give up on them. I know your friends used to give you shit over holding on so tight to Wyatt, but I was always so damn proud of you. He was just yours, and that was that, and now look what's happened. There's strength in that kind of loyalty, Harper Girl. Now you go get your mountains and keep us updated. We'll all be rooting for you here."

SIXTEEN

Martin glided out of the back office of the mine shop with an extra pep in his step. And was he whistling? Kane gave Wyatt a he's-finally-lost-his-mind look and dropped the sack of mine dirt in the metal bin along the wall.

Martin practically danced around the table of giant crystals for sale, backed up a step with a goofy look on his face, did a little twirl, and pranced sideways to Wyatt.

"Are you having a stroke?" he asked, concerned.

"It's payday." Martin twirled his wrist and offered Wyatt an envelope.

"It's definitely not. Payday is Friday." And whatever game Martin was playing, Wyatt wasn't interested. All he wanted to do was go back home to Harper.

Martin shoved the envelope against Wyatt's chest. "Just open it."

"Fine," he muttered, setting down the bundle of sand sacks. With a put-upon sigh, he ripped open the envelope flap and wrestled out the folded piece of paper.

W,

Hide and seek and it's your turn first. Count to 1010 and come find me. Oh, and wear your eatin' pants. I'm making us dinner and I probably won't burn it, pew pew. (dragon joke)

H

Wyatt jacked his confused gaze up to Martin. "Did Harper come by here?"

"Yep." The old man was practically bouncing on the balls of his feet.

"Why didn't you call me? We could've rushed."

"She didn't want me to. Don't worry about the

rest. I'll unload everything."

Kane piped up in a grumpy snarl, "He means I'll unload everything."

Martin pointed like Kane had won some contest. "Exactly. Bye, Wyatt. See you tomorrow, bright and early."

"Okaaay," Wyatt murmured. Baffled, he turned back at the door to make sure his boss wasn't in fact having some sort of episode, but the hunch-backed balding man stood there grinning like a happy gargoyle, so Wyatt shrugged at Kane and made his way out past the tourists sifting through dirt.

He was filthy from working up at the mine most of the day, but unable to resist the promise of seeing Harper and hearing that pretty humming sound vibrating from her chest again, he passed up his house, a prospect of a shower, and gunned it straight to Martin's property.

The gate was wide open. He pulled on through and came to a hard stop in front of 1010. The sun had set behind the mountains, and dim evening light made the autumn-painted woods seem other-worldly. But that wasn't what had his heart thumping in his chest. Two lit, flickering lanterns sat invitingly on the porch, one on either side of the door, which was open wide.

Wyatt shut the truck door quietly and made his way up the stairs. And when he reached the doorway, he was stunned into stillness. The scent of seasoned steak and lemon pepper asparagus brought an instant rumble to his belly. She had an old radio plugged into the wall, and a love song filled the small cabin with soft notes. A blanket was spread on the floor, topped with a couple of beers and a bowl of late season strawberries. It was Harper that froze his breath in his chest, though.

She stood with her back to him, stirring something on the stove, swaying gently to the music. Her dark hair had been curled at the ends and hung down to the middle of her back. She wore dark, skin-tight jeans tucked into hiking boots, and a moss green sweater clung to her curves.

"So you know, I won't be cooking like this all the time," she said softly. Harper threw him a boner-inducing smile over her shoulder and pulled the pan off the stove. "This is a special occasion. I'll be setting up an online law practice that will keep me busy, so you're gonna have to get on that grill if you want to eat."

He chuckled and ducked his chin to his chest. "Noted. What's the special occasion?" Claiming marks, their reunion, his reconciliation with the boys...really, it could be a lot of things.

Harper busied herself with piling food onto two paper plates, then sashayed those sexy hips his way. She dipped her gaze like she had grown shy all the sudden, and the words seemed to stay lodged in her throat, even though she parted her lips like she wanted to speak.

Worry slithered through him. "Hey, what's wrong?"

"I suddenly don't know if I've done the right thing. Or if you will be mad. Maybe this won't be a celebration for you."

Wyatt strode over to her and gripped her elbows. "Whatever you've done, I won't be mad. Just tell me."

Harper ghosted him a glance with those gorgeous half-dragon eyes of hers. She set the plates on the blanket and reached into her front pocket. She handed him a folded piece of paper, then wrung her hands.

Wyatt didn't like this, didn't want her upset. His bear let off a low growl as he opened the damning piece of paper that was causing his mate's anxiety.

As he read the paperwork, a creeping numbness took him. Couldn't be. He looked up at Harper to make sure this wasn't some kind of joke. "Is this really an offer on the mountains?"

"Well, it's a copy of my offer. Martin's realtor has the original."

He pointed to the signatures at the bottom. "Martin signed this."

"Yeah," she whispered, her dark, delicate eyebrows arching with concern. "He accepted my offer today, and we're trying for a quick close. Two weeks. But...I just thought about what this could mean to you. Your bear chose this place, and I'm buying it out from under you."

Hope flared in his chest. Carefully, he asked, "Harper, what does this mean?"

"I can rescind my offer if your bear—"

"Tell me fast. What do these mountains mean to you?"

Harper pursed her lips and locked her wild gaze on his. And so softly, so quietly, she murmured,

"They're mine."

Wyatt covered his face in his hands because, goddamn, hearing those words was everything he could want.

"Are you mad?"

Wyatt shook his head and paced to the door, then back, overwhelmed.

"Are you hurt?"

Wyatt crushed her against his chest and lifted her off the ground, buried his face right near the place he'd bitten her last night. "Tell me this is real. Don't play with me right now."

Harper laughed and wrapped her arms around his neck. "I'm serious. I tried to leave today—"

Wyatt jerked to a stop. "What?"

"No." Harper cupped his cheeks gently. "Not really *leave* leave. I just wanted to see if I could."

"What happened?"

"I got to the bridge outside of Bryson City and couldn't go any farther. My dragon wouldn't let me."

"Why?"

She was grinning so big now.

"Harper, why?" he asked louder, desperate for her answer.

"Because I found my treasure."

"The land?"

"And you. I think it's a package deal. I can't leave you. I can't leave the mountains. This is home. *You* are home. I haven't had any seizures today. Only the happy humming."

It was working. Not the way he'd planned, but it was working. She'd bonded to the mountains, sealed the bond to him. Now, maybe she could be okay. Maybe she could stop hurting, and maybe he could keep her, not just until The Unrest took his mate, but for always.

The picnic dinner meant something different now. Something bigger. Harper had set up their first meal in 1010.

His muscles shook with relief as he held her. She'd never looked happier or more beautiful than in this moment, cupping his cheeks, searching his eyes. And there it was, that happy rumble in her chest.

He'd never thought a sound could mean so much, but this one was everything. It was the signal that all was right in her world, and thus, all was right in his.

Dragging her waist closer just to feel her, he kissed her hard, then softer and softer until he laid sipping pecks on her mouth. She was crying, and it wasn't like when he'd left all those years ago. It wasn't the ragged, heartbreaking, body-wrenching sobs he'd seen in his rearview mirror as he'd driven away.

This right here was Harper telling him silently that she was overwhelmed in a good way because she'd somehow found joy after everything she'd been through.

"You're the strongest woman I've ever met," he murmured.

And when she looked up at him, her differently shaped pupils contracting, she had the sweetest smile on her lips, the most adoring look in her eyes, and he was certain, in this moment, Fate had known what she was doing all along. He and Harper had paid their dues to be together. They hadn't given up or forced each other from their minds. They'd held on when there was almost nothing to grasp onto. Because the only way to tether a soul to another living being was if they did it together.

They'd both been stripped bare in their years apart, and then to find each other again and feel this depth of consuming reprieve?

Their journey to this moment mattered.

As they settled in to eat the food she'd prepared, Wyatt couldn't help the smile on his face because the soft music in the background was textured with her giggles and laughter as they talked. He couldn't drag his attention away from the curve of her lips and the small smile lines at the corners of her eyes. He was enamored with her dark lashes brushing her cheeks every time she got thoughtful and looked down, and he was stunned over and over whenever she graced him with her gaze. One brown eye that said she was soft, womanly, caring, vulnerable, and then her fiery blue one with the elongated pupil that said she could be a fire-breathing death-bringer to anyone who messed with her or the people she loved.

Loyal Harper, one of the last Bloodrunner Dragons, and she'd seen right through his grit and chosen him. *Him*. He was going to spend the rest of his life earning the devotion that pooled in her eyes.

He opened his mouth to tell her how beautiful she was, but the long, haunting note of a wolf sounded on the breeze. Wyatt stood quickly and strode to the door, threw it open as a second howl joined the first.

"The Valdoro Pack?" Harper asked from right behind him.

Headlights shone through the trees up ahead, and Wyatt bared his teeth as his thoughts rushed. A third wolf joined the song. His bear could handle four, maybe five wolves at a time.

"Stay here," he murmured.

Harper snorted. "Not likely."

Right. Harper had never been a sit-on-the-sidelines type of person.

A wave of fear and protectiveness took him. It was a new sensation and had been consuming him since he'd bitten her, but the second he made Harper feel like she needed protection, she'd likely char his hide and remind him she was no damsel in need of rescuing.

Wyatt led her to the yard and waited for the silver SUV to come to a stop in front of them.

A single man got out. He was tall, lithe, and stank of fur and dominance. His face was scarred on one side, like some animal had clawed him, and his eyes were churning silver under his crop of mussed, dark hair.

He came to a stop in front of his ride and

dragged his furious gaze down Wyatt's torso like he was measuring him up. "Wyatt James," he said in a snarly voice.

"Axton," Wyatt greeted in a dead voice.

"I said I want you out of my territory, not to make another offer on this place!" His words tapered into a snarl as the veins bulged in his neck.

Harper stepped forward out of the shadows behind Wyatt. "It's not your territory."

"I wasn't talking to you, bitch."

Wyatt canted his head, and now he couldn't take his eyes off Axton's throat. "Talk to her like that again, and I'll be separating your head from your body, dog."

"I have ten wolves behind me, and you are out here unprotected. Save your posturing, *bear*."

Wyatt blew out a sigh and shook his head. "You should think of the well-being of your pack and leave. Leave here, leave this land."

"It ain't your land! It's mine!"

"Wrong," Harper said. Her chest rattled with a long, prehistoric rumble that rattled the air around them and made it hard for Wyatt to draw a breath. A smattering of pops sounded, and Wyatt stumbled out of the way as Harper's green and gold dragon heaved out of her body. She was four times the size of his bear, and her wings stretched long enough to cover the clearing. Her eyes blazed with fury as she snaked her long, scaly neck toward Axton.

"Holy fuckin' shit," the alpha of the Valdoro Pack murmured as he backed away slowly, his neck arched all the way back to take in the towering dragon.

Wyatt tried to contain his laugh, really he did, but from the look of mingled anger and terror on Axton's face, he and his inner wolf were at war on what to do. Fight or flee, fight or flee.

The howling in the woods stopped. Harper sucked in a heaving breath and let off a roar that echoed off the mountains. She was so fiercely beautiful.

Harper leapt into the air, beating her wings as she aimed for the clouds above. Hurricane-strength winds made Wyatt splay his legs to keep upright and pinned Axton against his ride. Then she was up, gracefully arching her back as she searched for the wind currents she wanted.

For a moment, she was nothing but a massive shadow blocking out the stars. And then the fire rained down in a long line through the woods.

"W-what is she doing?" Axton asked. "Pack!"

"She ain't after your pack, so settle the fuck down." Wyatt turned slowly, watching her fire cease, only to resume again in another long line as she worked her way north along the territory's edge. A slow smile took his face, and he huffed a soft chuckle. "She's marking her territory. If she burns it, she earns it."

"That doesn't make sense," Axton said, his wild eyes locked on the powerful burst of flames lighting up the forest. "She hasn't closed on the land yet."

"Sorry, asshole. Them's the rules."

Harper dipped sharply, dove for the ground, then rose above the tree line again, trailing plumes of blackened earth from her mouth. She was eating ashes, just like her ancestors had fed on when they'd scorched the earth. She was consuming her mountains. Chills blasted up the back of Wyatt's neck.

As she disappeared around the first mountain and the night sky behind it glowed red again, Wyatt advised the alpha, "I suggest you take your pack and leave her territory. She's a fair woman, but mess with something she loves, and she'll burn every last one of you to the ground. Never come here again."

Axton let off a shrill whistle. Wyatt pulled his shirt off and prepared for a Change in case he was calling his Pack in to attack, but the glowing eyes in the woods backed away and disappeared into the night.

Axton swung his furious gaze to Wyatt. His face was so contorted with hatred, he barely looked human. "I heard what you did to the Queen of the Asheville Coven. You've made too many enemies now, bear. If we don't off you, the vamps will. Even dragons have to sleep." He spat on the ground and snarled out, "This ain't over." And then the alpha of the Valdoro Pack strode around the side of his SUV and fishtailed out of the yard, spewing dirt as he gunned it.

As Wyatt watched him leave, he linked his hands behind his head and gritted his teeth against the curses he wanted to spew. The wolf was right. Wyatt swung his attention to where Harper was working her way around the back of the mountains. They didn't have the numbers, and that put them at risk. It put Harper at risk.

His mate was as tough as her armor-like scales,

but she wasn't invincible.

And Wyatt would be damned if he let anything else happen to the woman he loved.

He still had work to do to make sure his mate was safe.

SEVENTEEN

Harper held onto Wyatt's taut waist as the four-wheeler under them bounced and bumped. They'd closed on the land today, paid in full, the financial aid was coming through for Martin, and the deed was now hers. She smiled against the strong planes of his back as he sped through the woods. "What happened to taking me out on a fancy fourteenth date in Asheville?"

"Fourteen? Woman, are you counting our dates?"

"Maybe."

Wyatt's deep chuckle reverberated off her cheek. "This will be better," he promised over his shoulder.

"Trust me."

And she did. Life with Wyatt over the past few weeks had been nothing short of magical. She hadn't had a single bloody nose or seizure. With each passing day, she'd grown stronger and more confident in her body. She'd grown to love her dragon again. She hadn't felt anything but undiluted happiness. And yesterday, Wyatt had driven with her over the bridge outside of Bryson City and gone as far as the airport near Asheville. She'd been fine, and the relief that she could leave her mountains and visit home again, as long as Wyatt was with her, was proof that he was a huge part of her treasure. Her dragon trusted him, but then, she always had.

Harper could smell the scorch marks now. The wind kicked the smoky scent of ash into the air, which meant they were nearing the property line. Axton and his Valdoro Pack had left, and the vamps were lying low. Though her instincts told her this was only the calm eye of the storm, she was bound and determined to enjoy every moment of peace with her mate. Butterflies drummed around her middle at that thought.

Wyatt was really hers now. The mark on her

shoulder was undeniable proof that she belonged to him, and he to her.

"Close your eyes," Wyatt murmured, cupping his hand over hers as she tightened her arms around his waist.

She'd always adored surprises, and Wyatt had been so good with them when they were kids. Thoughtful invites to parties, little gifts wrapped in newspaper and left on her doorstep, flowers when she least expected them. And now that same sweet thoughtfulness she'd loved in the boy was still present in the man.

Harper closed her eyes as he pulled the ATV to a stop. He helped her off and spun her slowly, angling her shoulders toward the scent of the scorch marks she'd made those weeks ago.

His short facial scruff brushed against her cheek as he rested his face right against hers and wrapped his arms around her middle. "Open your eyes, Harper," he whispered.

What she saw in front of her rendered her breathless. He'd brought her to the cliffs, right on the edge of their land. Beyond, the fall colors of rust red and burnt orange drifted across the valleys and mountains like ocean waves. But sitting on a row of black boulders, right on the edge of the cliffs, were three men her heart would know anywhere.

Aaron, Ryder, and Weston were there, talking low, shoulder to shoulder, looking every bit like they belonged.

"Did you invite them?" she asked.

Wyatt smiled against her cheek. "Yes. Today is a big day, and we should be celebrating with them."

Harper stepped into the clearing, and the moment her shoe hit the wild grass, Weston turned, a slight and ready smile on his face. The boys met her in the middle of the clearing.

"Tell her," Ryder said, his eyes on Weston and blazing the gold of his snowy owl.

"Tell me what?" she asked, instantly worried something had gone wrong.

Weston shifted his weight and adjusted the hat on his head. When he lifted his gaze to her, his eyes were the pitch black of his raven. "I've been having dreams."

"What about?"

"It's the same every night. I see the cabin, 1010, and you're standing inside. Your mouth is covered in blood, and I try to run inside to help you. But then you smile, and the red disappears. And right before I wake up, you say the same thing, every time."

That she knew of, Weston didn't dream like his father before him. He'd never had the sight, but recurring dreams were a big deal. "What do I say?"

Weston swallowed hard and murmured, "You tell me, 'Come home.'" Weston fell to his knees and angled his face, exposing his neck. "Alpha."

Harper rocked back on her heels as Ryder dropped to his knees beside him, angled his neck and murmured, "Alpha."

She bit her lip hard to keep her emotions inside as Aaron dropped down in front of her, his blazing silver eyes locked on hers and that wicked smile on his lips. "Alpha."

And when she looked over at Wyatt, just to see if this was his plan, if he'd asked them to do this, he kissed her gently, then dropped to his knees. His chest heaved with emotion as he angled his neck. "It was never my destiny to be alpha, Harper. It was yours."

Deep within her, a long, loud, satisfied humming sound vibrated through her entire body. Her dragon stretched, and tendrils of power unfurled within her. If she did this, she was owning that she was okay and strong enough to protect them, guide them. It was a declaration that she was unafraid of The Unrest taking her. It was expanding her treasure and an oath to protect the ones she loved with her life. The decision was an easy one now because she wasn't scared anymore.

A slow smile stretched her face as she felt them—thin bonds, barely there, linking her to each one of them. The wind picked up, whipping her hair about her face as she clenched her hands.

Ryder grinned like he could see her answer in her face. "Give us the order and make it official."

Harper blew out a long steadying breath and jerked her chin to the drop-off behind them. "Air-Ryder and Novak Raven...go jump off a cliff."

"Whoo!" Ryder yelled, stripping his shirt as he bolted for the cliff's edge. He threw out his hands in the final second, jumped, and disappeared over the edge. And a moment later, his massive snowy owl appeared above the rim, coasting along the currents.

Weston stood and hugged Harper up tight, and before he followed Ryder, he turned to Wyatt and said, "You did good." With a last smile for Harper, Weston sprinted for the cliff and jumped off. And then a raven with shiny black feathers beat his wings and glided beside the white owl with eyes the color of the sun.

Aaron stripped out of his clothes, and his muscles contracted in the instant before the massive blond grizzly exploded from him. He paced a tight circle around her, a soft, content rumble in his throat. And then there was Wyatt, standing slowly, such pride in his eyes.

She ran her hands up his chest, stood on her tiptoes, and pressed her lips to his. She squeezed her eyes closed, and the moisture that had built there spilled over onto her cheek. Easing back, Wyatt brushed her tear away with the pad of his thumb and whispered, "You saved me."

But he was so wrong. He was the one who had saved her. She would live because of the land he'd found, because of the claiming mark he'd given her, and because of the crew he'd built for her.

My crew.

Harper squeezed his hands, then undressed carefully, savoring the moment. When she was ready and the breeze whipped against her bare skin, she gave her mate one last grin and ran for the cliff. Her arms caught the wind as she leapt off the edge, and for a moment, she closed her eyes and fell. She'd been brought back from the brink of death by love. By devotion. She'd been jaded and had hated her dragon for clinging too tightly to things that didn't belong to her, but her inner animal had been right the entire time. If she'd given up on Wyatt, she wouldn't have been gifted this moment. Harper gave her dragon her body and flapped her wings once, arching her back as she blasted away from the ground and aimed for the clouds.

When she looked at Wyatt, he was standing on the edge of the cliff, watching her with the same smile he wore as a boy when he'd watched her Change. Then he hunched inward, and the bear she loved rippled from his body. As she rose higher, he and Aaron paced along the cliff ledge, eyes on her, waiting.

She circled higher above her mountains. Beneath her, the owl and the raven flew a wide circle above the grizzlies on the cliff, and this was it. This was the moment she would bind them all.

The bears roared, the owl and the raven cried out, and Harper inhaled deeply and bellowed with them.

She wouldn't be a victim of The Unrest, or fodder for vampires or wolves. She wouldn't be alone ever again.

No longer was she a woman who didn't belong.

No longer was she the dragon without a treasure.

Now and for always, she would be the keeper of these mountains, and the alpha of the Bloodrunner Crew.

Want more of these characters?

Bloodrunner Dragon is the first book in a five book series based in Harper's Mountains.

Check out these other books from T. S. Joyce.

Bloodrunner Bear
(Harper's Mountains, Book 2)

Air Ryder
(Harper's Mountains, Book 3)

Novak Raven
(Harper's Mountains, Book 4)

Blackwing Dragon
(Harper's Mountains, Book 5)

Read on for a sneak peek of Bloodrunner Bear.

Sneak Peek

Bloodrunner Bear
(Harper's Mountains, Book 2)

Chapter One

"Fire department, call out!" Aaron Keller yelled as he ducked under a thick plume of smoke and frantically searched the tile floor of a large bathroom. There was still one woman unaccounted for according to the landlord, and this place was going up in flames fast.

The roar of the fire was only eclipsed by Aaron's heavy breathing inside his mask. Flames licked at his turnout gear as he passed a coat closet that was actively burning. That could be trouble if this part of the wall collapsed when he was in the back of the small rental duplex.

"Aaron, fall back," Chief said from the safety of the street outside.

Aaron's partner, Mark, had been over the radio, updating the boss man on how bad it was in here and how much time they had left, because yeah, after a while firefighters got an instinct for that. They understood the behavior of fire on an intimate level. Aaron knew Chief was right, but he had one more room, and he'd be damned if a woman burned because he left too early. Not today. Losing people stuck with his inner bear. He was supposed to protect people, not let them die.

"Fire department, call out!" Aaron yelled louder as he shoved the final bedroom door open with his shoulder. The back of the room was a solid wall of yellow flames, roiling like waves up toward the ceiling, the fire searching for air, seeking oxygen. With the closed windows in here, there wasn't much left.

There she was. A woman in a robe lay on the floor, motionless. Shit.

Mark was yelling into the radio for him to evacuate, his voice too damn loud for Aaron's oversensitive ears. Ignoring his partner, he bolted for the woman. The ceiling was coming down, and while he had fire resistant clothing and shifter healing, if this woman was still alive, she wouldn't survive a cave-in. Aaron skidded on his knees and threw himself on top of her.

The roar of the rafters hitting the floor around them was overwhelming, and something heavy struck him on the back. The pain was instant—too much weight, too much pressure—but Mark was right there, pulling away debris. Aaron could tell from the heat easing off his body. The instant he was able, Aaron sat back on his knees, yanking the woman with him, and then he and Mark bolted out of the blazing inferno. The ambulance was just pulling up, but the firefighters were trained paramedics, and Aaron knew what to do in the moments before the team reached them on the sidewalk out front. He set the woman down, stripped off his mask and gloves, and felt for a pulse. It was there, but faint. He put his cheek in front of her face but couldn't feel a breath. He tilted her head back, plugged her nose, and prepared to do mouth-to-mouth resuscitation but Aric dropped down beside him, shoving him out of the way. "Back off, shithead. You'll kill her."

Kill her? Who had just pulled her out of the burning house? Fuckin' vampire. Aaron hated Aric, but there wasn't room for a brawl right here in the dark street as they lost this lady to smoke inhalation.

Aaron paced, a snarl in his throat as his instincts to protect her from Aric warred with his need to help with the hoses.

"Aaron, do work," Chief demanded.

Chest heaving, he kept his eyes averted and nodded. His eyes would be bright green-gold right now, and Chief always told him and Aric to keep their "supernatural shit" to themselves. A month working for the Bryson City Fire Department, and Aaron was pretty sure Chief would never accept the bear side of him. It wasn't like in his last firehouse in Breckenridge. There, half the crew had been bear shifters, and no one cared about him exposing his inner animal. They were accepting, but here, everything was different. He still felt off-balance.

Aric pushed the heel of his palm against her chest one last time, then stopped and set his ear over her mouth as if checking for breath. His lips moved like he was mumbling something, but Aric's sandy brown hair had fallen in front of his face, covering his murmured words. The woman gasped for breath and coughed over and over. And though he might hate Aric for what he was, for the scars Aaron now bore on his neck, and for what his coven had tried to do to his

227

alpha, he couldn't deny the fact that Aric was good at raising humans from near death.

Aric slid an oxygen mask over her face, and the paramedics scattered toward a pair of coughing teens on their hands and knees in the yard of the connected house.

"Aaron!" Aric barked out, his eyes full of horror.

"What?"

"My baby," the woman choked out through the mask, her eyes vacant. "Where's my baby?"

Fuck! Aaron pulled on his mask and sprinted for the open doorway. The fire hadn't reached the front of the house yet. A nursery. He must've missed a nursery.

"Aaron, I said fall back!" Chief yelled over the radio. "Get your ass outside now! That's an order. Fuck. Mark! Bring him back!"

Living room, kitchen, two bedrooms, two bathrooms, no nursery. The ceiling was raining burning sheetrock and embers. The smoke was too thick near the bedrooms. Maybe the baby had been sleeping in the woman's room? Why the fuck didn't she have the baby in her arms?

Hose water blasted through the living room

window onto the flames against the back wall, and Aaron covered his mask from the spray. He had to keep a good visual, and the smoke was already making it hard. There was no crying.

Please be okay. Please be where I can reach you.

In the hallway, the rafters caved, and burning debris landed hard on his forearm, yanking him down. His arm was pinned under him, against the searing materials. So hot. Burning. Franticly, Aaron yanked his arm out from under the rubble and backed away. The way to the bedroom was blocked now. *The baby.*

A rough hand grabbed his turnout gear and pulled him backward. Mark. "There's no one left!" he yelled through the radio. "You'll get yourself killed for nothing!"

Aaron shoved off him. "There's a baby!"

Through his mask, Mark's eyes were scared as he looked up at the wall of flames above them. The human had a family—a wife and two kids. He was young, three years out of Fire Academy. He was a good one. Mark wouldn't leave without him, and now it was the baby or Mark. Aaron's heartbeat was roaring in his ears as he tossed one last glance back to the bedroom. He could just make out the walls coming down, and he knew it was too late.

He grabbed Mark's shoulder, and together they ran from the house. Now, he was going to have to break it to the woman that he'd failed her. He'd done this before, told families about their loved ones he hadn't been strong enough, or fast enough, to save. This was his least favorite part of the job. She would look up at him, her eyes hollow, because deep down she would already know he hadn't pulled off a miracle. Even though he didn't have her baby in his arms, she would still ask him, and his answer would destroy her entire world. And he would carry that burden, along with all the others, until the day he drew his last breath.

But when he saw the woman, she was smiling and looked relieved. What the hell? Maybe she was in shock. He cast Mark a quick glance to make sure he was out safe with him. His partner was talking low to Chief. Aaron made his way through the paramedics and approached the woman slowly.

"Thank you for saving me," she said, her voice scratchy from the smoke.

"But...your baby. I couldn't get to it."

A frown of utter confusion commandeered her face. With a slight shake of her head, she whispered, "I don't have baby."

"But...you said..."

Horror washed over Aaron as his arm began throbbing in rhythm to his pounding pulse. He looked down at his searing arm. The fire had eaten through his jacket, and he could make out the angry red blisters of his ruined skin beneath. In a moment of clarity, the memory of Aric's whispers while resuscitating the woman flashed through his mind. It wasn't some incantation he'd been uttering to keep her from death, but mind-manipulation.

Aaron pulled off his mask. Fuck his gold eyes and who saw them. He blinked slowly and raised his furious gaze to Aric who was on the hose with a couple of the others from their station. Aric was watching him. A predatory smile spread across his face as his eyes turned black as coal. Fuckin' vampire.

Rage pulsed in Aaron's veins before he charged him. He was to Aric in a moment, pummeling him, his fist shattering against the asshole's stony jaw, but Aaron didn't care. "You could've gotten me killed!"

Stupid fucking smile on Aric's face. "That was the

point, Bloodrunner."

"Aaron, stop it!" Chief yelled from behind.

They were trying to pull him off the vamp, but Aaron wouldn't be moved. He was searching the ground around them for something wooden, something he could shove through Aric's chest cavity and kill him with. This was too much, too much for his inner monster to let pass.

"Kill her."

"What?" Aaron shook his head. That sounded like his bear. Kill her? Kill who?

"Kill the dragon. Kill, kill, kill. Kill your unworthy alpha. Kill the dragon."

Aaron shook his head hard. *Stop it, Bear.*

"Kill the Bloodrunner Dragon so you can become alpha."

It was Aric. Aric was manipulating his animal. Aaron slammed the King of the Asheville Coven against the concrete, and there it was, the first crack in Aric's poker face. He winced in pain, so Aaron slammed him against the driveway over and over, a snarl in his chest. His arm hurt so fucking bad, but he would break his own bones to kill this asshole for what he'd done. For what he was suggesting.

Aaron loved Harper. She was his cousin. She was good. Maybe she was the best person he'd ever known. The best alpha. Good, good, good.

Aaron opened his mouth and roared his fury.

He would stake Aric a thousand times before he would hurt a hair on the Bloodrunner Dragon's head.

About the Author

T.S. Joyce is devoted to bringing hot shifter romances to readers. Hungry alpha males are her calling card, and the wilder the men, the more she'll make them pour their hearts out. She werebear swears there'll be no swooning heroines in her books. It takes tough-as-nails women to handle her shifters.

Experienced at handling an alpha male of her own, she lives in a tiny town, outside of a tiny city, and devotes her life to writing big stories. Foodie, wolf whisperer, ninja, thief of tiny bottles of awesome smelling hotel shampoo, nap connoisseur, movie fanatic, and zombie slayer, and most of this bio is true.

Bear Shifters? Check

Smoldering Alpha Hotness? Double Check

Sexy Scenes? Fasten up your girdles, ladies and gents, it's gonna to be a wild ride.

For more information on T. S. Joyce's work,
visit her website at
www.tsjoyce.com

SLIME!

Racehorse for Young Readers books may be purchased in bulk at special discounts for sales promotion, corporate gifts, fund-raising, or educational purposes. Special editions can also be created to specifications. For details, contact the Special Sales Department, Skyhorse Publishing, 307 West 36th Street, 11th Floor, New York, NY 10018 or info@skyhorsepublishing.com.

Racehorse for Young Readers™ is a pending trademark of Skyhorse Publishing, Inc.®, a Delaware corporation.

Visit our website at www.skyhorsepublishing.com.

10 9 8 7 6 5 4 3 2 1

Library of Congress Cataloging-in-Publication Data is available on file.

Cover design by Michael Short
Cover photograph by iStockphoto
Interior photography by Trisha Haas

ISBN: 978-1-63158-216-5
eISBN: 978-1-63158-217-2

Printed in the United States of America

SLIME!

DO-IT-YOURSELF PROJECTS TO MAKE AT HOME

TRISHA HAAS AND CHARLOTTE HAAS

CONTAINS INSTRUCTIONS FOR MORE THAN 20 BORAX-FREE RECIPES!

FOR YOUNG READERS

TABLE OF CONTENTS

AUTHOR'S NOTE

For the past ten years spent as a creative blogger, I have been one of the many voices providing messy play inspiration to the online parenting community. I personally believe that by encouraging creativity and getting our hands a little dirty, we are helping our children problem solve and learn—all while having tons of fun. In our household, slime has been a big part of that. Customizing combinations of colors and using a variety of glues for new consistencies make the experimentation process even more exciting. My hope is that the recipes and tips in this book will inspire you and your kids to get creative and have a blast with these fun and messy projects!

INTRODUCTION

Crafting recipes, unlike food recipes, are about finding out what works for you. They are meant to challenge you to solve a problem. As you start to understand slime and what it does, do not be afraid to step outside the bounds of the recipes within this book and experiment to create your own.

Before you get started, here are the items most commonly used:

- Elmer's white glue (I highly suggest using white glue by the gallon, which can be purchased on Amazon)

- Elmer's clear glue

- Fine glitter crafting glue (Most commonly found in craft stores)

- Liquid starch (This will say "Good for Crafting" on a blue bottle)

- Icing food coloring (Works very well for a colorant without diluting glue)

- Acrylic paint (Metallic is fine)

- Glitter (Fine/Medium)

Disclaimer: Although this book uses the term "recipe," projects are not edible! They are not meant to be eaten!

BASIC SLIME RECIPES

Let's get started!

It is important to note that the type of glue you use, as well as the items you use to color your slime, will have an impact on how it feels and flows. Not all white glues, clear glues, or even glitter glues are created in the same way; therefore, it can take some time to understand which product you should use to achieve the desired effect. As you become familiar with these basic slime recipes and your knowledge of the goo grows, it will become easier to borrow and reuse these ideas and techniques to make more creative and fun slimes.

WHITE GLUE SLIME

Consistency: Thick, Flows at medium speed

This is the most commonly used form of slime. Its recipe is also the easiest to customize, due to its neutral white color and—depending on your portions and technique—its drastic changes in consistency. White glue is typically available in most stores, making it the most convenient as well.

You can use this basic recipe to make large batches of slime for nearly any project, including those that incorporate different colors. For the sake of adding some color to an otherwise colorless slime, the recipe that follows includes the ingredients to make traditional green slime.

For this project, you will need:

- 1/2 cup white glue
- 1/3 cup liquid starch
- Icing food coloring (blue and yellow)

INSTRUCTIONS:

1. Measure out 1/2 cup of white glue and pour it into a cup or large bowl. Add 2–3 drops of icing food coloring and stir until you have the right shade of green.

2. Add 1/3 cup of liquid starch and combine. Your glue should start to form into slime almost immediately.

3. Pull out the glue and begin passing it back and forth between your hands, stretching and kneading as you go. If there is any starch left in the bowl or cup you used, dip your slime back in to make sure it absorbs all of the remaining starch. This takes approximately 3–4 minutes.

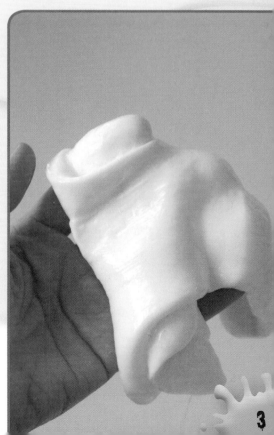

PAINT SLIME

Consistency: Thick, Flows slowly

When making slime, many people complain that it turns out either too thick or too runny. The wonderful thing about slime recipes is that you can adjust the portions to achieve your desired consistency. The downside is that it takes some experimentation; varying just one ingredient can change the entire result. To help guide you through the process, please refer to the following instructions.

For this project, you will need:

- 1/2 cup white glue
- 1/3 cup liquid starch
- 2 teaspoons acrylic paint colors

INSTRUCTIONS:

1. Measure out 1/2 cup of white glue into a cup or large bowl. Add 2 teaspoons of acrylic paint to glue and stir until color is uniform.

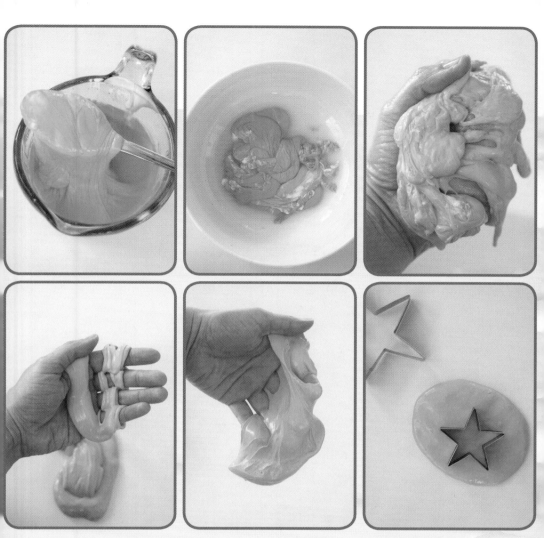

2. Add 1/3 cup of liquid starch and stir. Your glue should start to form into a clump quickly.

3. Pull out glue and begin passing it back and forth between your hands, stretching and kneading as you go. The slime will feel very sticky and goopy at this stage.

4. Continue passing between your hands, stretching and pulling the slime like taffy. You can get creative by wrapping it around your hands or stretching it in different directions, folding the ends over each other. The more you stretch, the more starch is

absorbed, which will help the slime reach the perfect consistency!

5. Hold your slime upside down. If it starts to slowly fall on its own and no longer sticks to your hands, it's perfect!

TIP:

If you add additional paint to get a specific color, you may need to reduce the amount of starch being added to balance out the consistency.

CLEAR GLUE SLIME

Consistency: Thick, Flows slowly, Stretches thinly well

When making slime, it can be hard to know if you are headed in the right direction, as it goes through many stages before it reaches that perfect consistency. Find out what you can expect while making slime that includes a clear glue base in the following recipe.

For this project, you will need:

- 2/3 cup clear glue
- Approximately 1 teaspoon fine glitter
- 1/3 cup liquid starch

INSTRUCTIONS:

1. Add your clear glue to a bowl. Stir in approximately 1 teaspoon of fine glitter.

2. Add 1/3 cup of liquid starch and stir for about 1 minute until it is completely absorbed. Your slime will start to form, but will still be very wet.

3. Pick up your slime—which will be sticky—and start passing it back and forth between your hands, twirling it around and around with your fingers. By doing this, the slime will start to thicken.

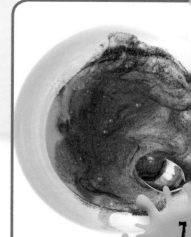

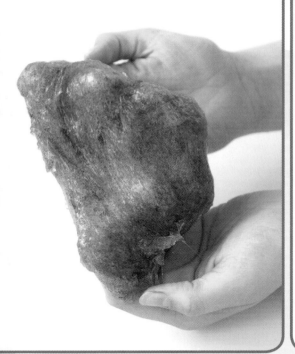

4. Once your slime is a firmer consistency, start stretching it out thinly. It is now ready to use.

PINK GLITTER SLIME

Consistency: Sticky, Flows at medium speed

This is a perfect glitter slime, with a gorgeous flow and a beautiful stretch. It varies from fine glitter crafting slime, as the ratio of glue to glitter is higher and therefore sticks together very well. Please note that the consistency is different in all slimes.

For this project, you will need:

- 2/3 cup Elmer's classic glitter glue (pink)
- 3 tablespoons liquid starch

INSTRUCTIONS:

1. To make the most perfect glitter slime, use Elmer's glitter glue. This brand of glue consists of colored translucent glue with a mix of sparkles. You will not need additional food or icing color for this slime.

2. Measure out 2/3 cup of your glitter glue.

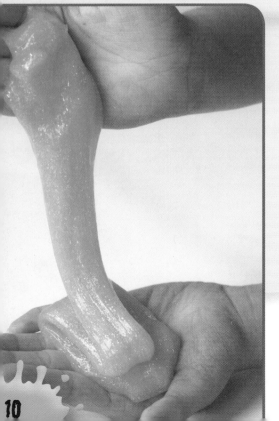

3. Add 3 tablespoons of liquid starch.

4. Stir together until your glue starts to clump up and the starch begins to be absorbed.

5. Pull the newly formed slime out and begin kneading and pulling the slime like you would taffy. Your slime will start out with a wetter consistency and begin forming into the perfect slime the more you play with it. This should take approximately 3–4 minutes.

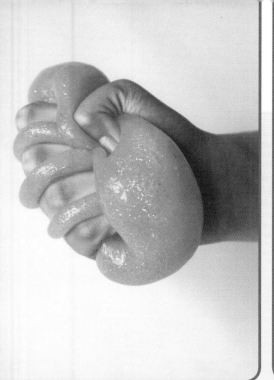

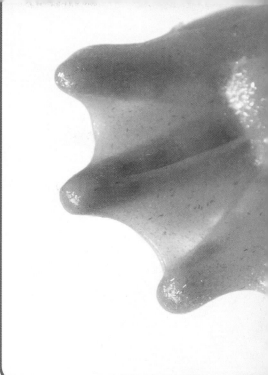

TIP:

If you find that your slime is still a bit sticky, make sure you used all the starch in the measuring cup. Simply dip your slime into any leftover liquid starch and continue kneading. If you need to, add small increments of starch one teaspoon at a time until slime is formed to your liking.

FINE GLITTER SLIME (PURPLE)

Consistency: Gooey, Flows quickly

Slime made with fine glitter crafting glue is more of an oozing, sticky slime that quickly moves between your fingers. Due to the massive amounts of fine glitter in this type of slime, it's a lot messier in your hands—which also makes it a lot more fun! While this slime is typically only good for a single use (given that it does not store well), it is still incredibly fun and great sensory play.

For this project, you will need:

- 1/2 cup pre-made fine glitter crafting glue (purple)

- 1 cup liquid starch

INSTRUCTIONS:

1. Fine glitter glue is mostly available at craft stores in tall bottles. It's made almost entirely of sparkly glitter, giving the starch less glue to grab onto, thus making it more of an oozy slime. Fine glitter glue comes in a variety of colors (your slime will be the color of the glue bottle you purchase).

TIP:

Worth noting is that fine glitter crafting glue comes in gorgeous colors that are difficult to duplicate using your own coloring, so this type of glue is a must for this beautiful slime.

2. Measure out 1/2 cup of fine glitter glue into a measuring cup. Pour into a large bowl.

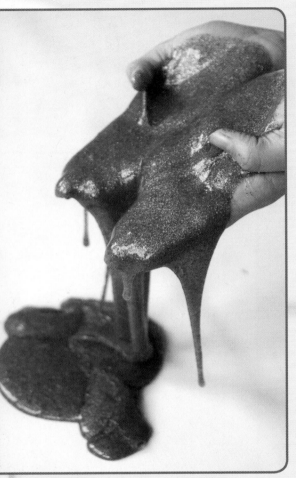

3. Add 1 cup of liquid starch, 1/3 cup at a time, mixing as you go.

4. Stir together until your glue starts to clump up and the starch begins to be fully absorbed.

5. Once the starch begins to absorb into the glue, pull out the mass and pass between your hands, kneading the glue and starch together. The process on this slime is longer, taking 5–7 minutes to be fully formed and ready for play. This slime will not form into a solid ball like other slimes and is easier to play with on a vinyl sheet.

Note: As previously mentioned, this is a one-time slime and does not store well. If you store it, it will eventually breakdown and liquefy.

IDEAS & INSPIRATION

Now that you have these basic slime recipes down, it's time to get creative! Take your slime to a whole new level by mixing colors, textures, and glue types. Here are a few ideas to help inspire you to take your slime one step further and make something incredible.

RAINBOW SLIME

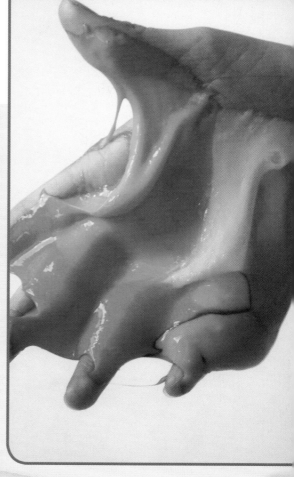

Consistency: Thick, Flows at medium speed

There is nothing more dazzling than rainbow slime! Combining gorgeous colors, rainbow slime is such a beautiful sensory experience that offers a wide variety of fun. I typically use traditional rainbow colors, but feel free to alter this recipe and go with your little one's favorite colors. (Even better, use your own. Make slime fun for you, too!)

For each color in this slime, you will need:

- 1/2 cup white glue
- 1/3 cup liquid starch
- Icing food coloring (red, yellow, blue)

INSTRUCTIONS:

1. This is a traditional slime recipe made with white glue. It is the easiest to make and most foolproof of the more complex slimes.

2. Measure out 1/2 cup of white glue and pour it into a cup or large bowl. Add 2–5 drops of icing food coloring and stir until the colors are fully formed. I use icing food coloring, as it does not thin out your glue.

3. Add 1/3 cup of liquid starch and stir. Your glue should start to form into slime almost immediately.

4. Pull out the glue and begin passing back and forth between your hands, stretching and kneading as you go. If there is any starch left in the bowl or cup, dip your slime back in to make sure it absorbs anything residual. This takes approximately 3–4 minutes per color.

5. Repeat steps for red, orange, yellow, green, and blue in separate bowls.

6. Now, once you have created all five colors, you can begin to build the rainbow. Place one strand of each slime in your hands, one color at a time, and let them drip into a rainbow. Please note that the more you play with the slime, the more the colors will begin to blend, eventually leading to one solid color (typically blue or purple). This is the end result of all multi-colored slime recipes. Store the slime in a Ziploc baggie or sealed container for up to one week.

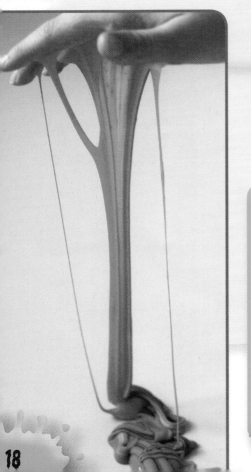

TIP:

If the slime seems stringy and unable to form into one lump after starch is mixed in completely, simply put your slime down on a glass plate or in a glass bowl and let it expand and stretch out. In approximately 2–3 minutes, once it has stretched out on its own, the slime should be one cohesive unit.

GALAXY SLIME

Consistency: Gooey, Flows very quickly

Inspired by the colors of the stars, this slime recipe bears a stunning resemblance to the bewitching night sky, with all of its deep purples and blues. Galaxy slime is truly as messy as they come and will give you a totally different experience than solid slimes, making it really fun to play with on reusable crafting vinyl. The consistency of fine glitter crafting glue allows the slime to fully blend together, making a beautiful and gorgeous galaxy of glimmering stars.

For this project, you will need:

- 1/2 cup fine glitter crafting glue for each color (purple, black, and blue)
- 1 cup liquid starch

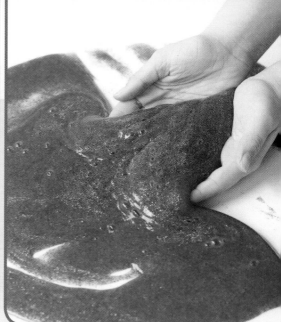

INSTRUCTIONS:

1. Grab three separate mixing bowls. Measure out 1/2 cup of your first glitter glue color and pour into bowl. Repeat with the two other colors, rinsing and drying your measuring cup in between.

2. One at a time, add 1/3 cup of liquid starch to each bowl. Complete one set of slime before moving onto the next.

3. Starch should be fully absorbed at this point. Pull out each of the slimes and pass them back and forth between your hands. The glue and starch have to work together to create its gooey consistency. This type of slime takes a little longer to form, as all fine glitter glue slimes do. Expect 5–7 minutes for each color.

4. Once your three colors are formed, your slime will be an oozy, sticky slime. Pour the slime out, one color at a time, onto a vinyl drop, which makes for easy clean up. Experiment with adding colors together, passing between your hands, and letting the slime drip from your fingers. The colors will begin to combine over time into one color, but will still be quite beautiful.

Note: This slime cannot be stored.

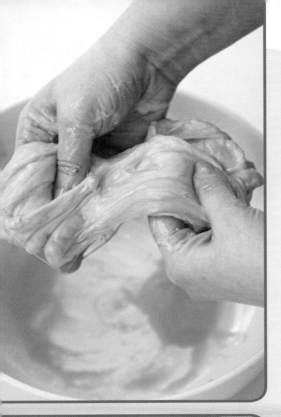

METALLIC PAINT SLIME (BLUE)

Consistency: Thick, Flows slowly

This type of slime is thick, super simple to play with, and mess free. The glue used to color the slime helps create a stronger bond; therefore, it can be passed between hands without the stickiness that other slimes have. It also has a slower flow and takes longer to stretch.

For this project, you will need:

- 1/2 cup white glue
- 1/3 cup liquid starch
- 2 teaspoons metallic acrylic paint colors

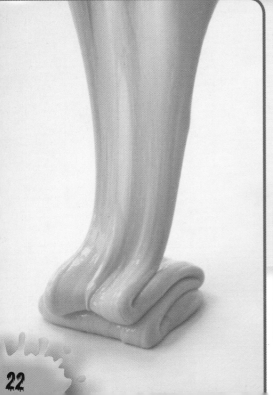

TIP:

Use this recipe for party favors and put in small containers with lids or baggies to pass out. Be sure to specify that it is not edible!

INSTRUCTIONS:

1. Measure out 1/2 cup of white glue and pour it into a cup or large bowl. Add 2 teaspoons of metallic acrylic paint and stir until color is uniform.

2. Then add 1/3 cup of liquid starch and stir. Your glue should start to form into a clump quickly.

3. Pull out the glue and begin passing back and forth between your hands, stretching and kneading as you go. If there is any starch left in the bowl or cup you used, dip your slime back in to make sure it absorbs any residual starch.

4. This slime is low flow. Kneading it to the right consistency can take about 4 minutes. Wrap it around your hands, fingers, and wrists to test stretch.

Note: The more paint you add, the slower the flow will be. If you add additional paint to get a specific color, you may need to reduce your starch.

TIE-DYE SLIME

Consistency: Thick, Flows at medium speed

Tie-dye slime flaunts a beautiful combination of colors that drip into a fun mix! To create tie-dye slime, set aside half of the colors used to create "rainbow slime"—a vibrant combination of red, orange, yellow, green, and blue. If you are making this for the first time, proceed with the following instructions.

For each color in this slime, you will need:

- 1/2 cup white glue
- 1/3 cup liquid starch
- Icing food coloring

INSTRUCTIONS:

1. Grab 5 mixing bowls or large cups. Measure out 1/2 cup of white glue in each. Add 2–5 drops of icing food coloring and stir until each

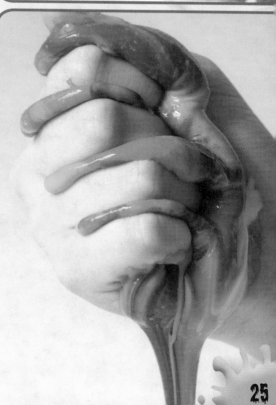

color is fully formed. I use icing colors so it does not thin out the glue.

2. Add 1/3 cup of liquid starch and stir. Your glue should start to form into slime almost immediately.

3. Pull out the glue and begin passing it back and forth between your hands, stretching and kneading as you go. If there is any starch left in the bowls or cups you used, dip your slime back in to make sure it absorbs anything residual. This should take approximately 3–4 minutes. Put each color back in its respective bowl until it's ready to use.

4. Tie-dye: To create this look, you simply need to start combining the colors together. Lay down each slime in your hand, with a bit of each color side by side. Be careful to use close to the same amount of each color. Squeeze your hand together and let the

slime drip down. Pick up the slime and re-peat. Now, gather your slime and open your hand. If one color is dominating, peel some of the slime from the bottom of your hand to the top. Watch the beautiful colors drip and form tie-dye over your fingers.

Note: As you play, the colors will continue to combine over time and eventually form a single color.

DOUBLE BATCH GLITTER SLIME

Consistency: Thick, Flows slowly, Stretches well

Unlike slime that includes glitter right in the glue, this glitter slime is customizable so you can mix your favorite glitter into the formula to create a sparkly concoction of your own choosing! This formula also stretches thinly very well and holds its shape.

For this project, you will need:

- 1 1/3 cup clear glue
- 2/3 cup liquid starch
- 1 tablespoon medium grain glitter

INSTRUCTIONS:

1. Add 1 1/3 cup of clear glue to a bowl.

2. Dump in 1 tablespoon of medium glitter and mix well. The glitter should dominate the bowl.

3. Now add 2/3 cup of liquid starch and stir.

4. Once slime begins to form, you can remove it from the bowl and knead between your hands. Make sure all the starch is absorbed by continuously dipping or swirling slime in the bowl. The more you stretch the slime, the more pliable it will become for play.

Fun to note: We created this recipe by accident. While trying to sprinkle in a tiny bit of glitter into clear glue, the lid fell off and the entire bottle dumped in!

PRETZEL SLIME

Consistency: Thick, Flows slowly, Stretches well

Clear slimes are fantastic for creating a twisted slime where the colors mix together. Pretzel slime is especially fun for younger kids, who will enjoy playing with a slime that has a slower flow and multiple color combinations.

This project requires two separate slimes to twist together! Therefore, you will need the following ingredients to create both:

First color:

- 2/3 cup clear glue
- 1 tablespoon of medium glitter
- 1/3 cup liquid starch

Second color:

- 2/3 cup clear glue
- Sprinkle of fine glitter
- 1/3 cup liquid starch

INSTRUCTIONS:

1. Add 2/3 cup of clear glue to a bowl.

2. Dump in 1 tablespoon of medium glitter and mix well. The glitter should dominate the bowl. (For the second color, repeat steps 1-3, but only use a sprinkle of fine glitter in Step 2.)

3. Now add 1/3 cup of liquid starch and stir.

4. Once both slimes have been created, roll out each color like dough and fold each strand together like a pretzel. Experiment with color changes. Due to the nature of how thick this slime is, it's easier to play with without colors mixing too quickly. This slime also stretches out very thin, so practice stretching on your hands or arms. Store in Ziploc bag.

Note: When creating clear glue slime, it is easiest to combine the starch and glue in a bowl, stirring for approximately 1 minute until the starch is completely soaked up by the glue. Then pick up your newly formed slime and begin stretching and kneading it. This slime starts out super wet, so do not be alarmed. After approximately 2 minutes, the slime will begin to thicken. Stretch it out to see its properties.

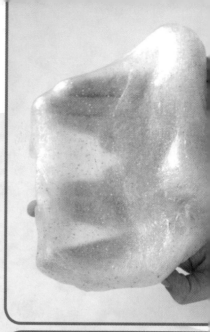

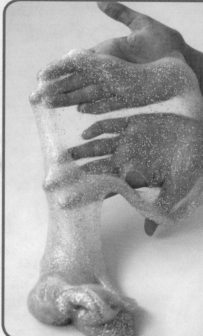

SNOT SLIME

Consistency: Thick, Flows at a medium speed

Whenever I think of slime, I always think of green slime! Green slime is the most commonly used in movies and TV shows, and often resembles snot (hence the name given to this slime). The recipe below creates a slime that flows at a medium speed, which allows for stretching gorgeous, long strings. However, the slime is still malleable enough to maintain its ability to recombine. The white glue used has a great stretch as well, so do not be afraid to double batch this one.

For this project, you will need:

- 1/2 cup white glue
- 1/3 cup liquid starch
- Icing food coloring

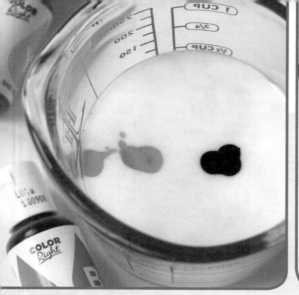

INSTRUCTIONS:

1. Measure out 1/2 cup of white glue and pour it into a cup or large bowl. Add 2-3 drops of icing food coloring (blue and yellow) and stir until you have the right green.

2. Add 1/3 cup of liquid starch and combine. Your glue should start to form into slime almost immediately.

3. Pull out the glue and begin passing back and forth between your hands, stretching and kneading it as you go. If there is any starch left in the bowl or cup, dip your slime back in to make sure it absorbs any residual liquid. This takes approximately 3-4 minutes.

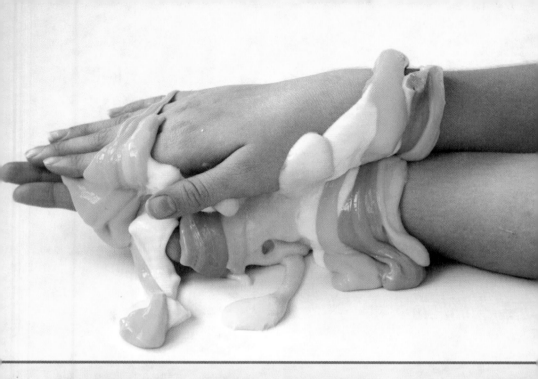

UNICORN POOP SLIME

Consistency: Thick, Flows at a medium speed

Unicorn poop slime is the most popular slime recipe on my website. I wanted to include a variation of this slime here so you could enjoy it as well. On MomDot.com, the unicorn poop slime is made with pastels, but this recipe creates a brighter, cheerier version by incorporating a combination of color changes and by using starch over borax.

For each color in this slime, you will need:

- 1/2 cup white glue

- 1/3 cup liquid starch

- Icing food coloring (yellow, orange, pink, teal, and purple)

INSTRUCTIONS (REPEAT FOR EACH COLOR):

1. Measure out 1/2 cup of white glue and pour it into a cup or large bowl. Add 2–3 drops of icing food coloring to achieve the color you want. If you are looking for pastels, you may need to add a minimal amount of icing food coloring (I use a toothpick to drip) to keep the colors light. To make the colors dark like shown, simply use the food coloring as directed. (Take note that dark colors like blue and red will become very dark quickly.)

2. Add 1/3 cup of liquid starch and combine. Your glue should start to form into slime almost immediately.

3. Pull out glue and begin passing it back and forth between your hands, stretching and kneading as you go. If there is any residual starch left in the bowl or cup, dip your slime back in to make sure it absorbs anything leftover. This takes approximately 3–4 minutes.

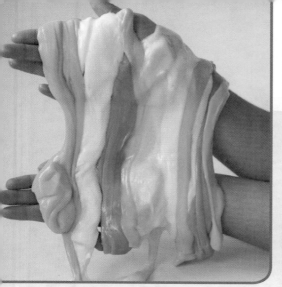

TIP:

If you prefer to do some advanced preparation, in separate bowls you can simultaneously measure out the glue and coloring for each color before adding the starch and kneading. This is a faster alternative to making one slime at a time. If you choose this method, be sure to only add starch to one bowl at a time and to complete the slime creation process before moving on to the next color. If you pour the starch into each bowl before completing the slime process, the slime will get stringy as it rests and mixes. However, if you do happen to add starch too early in the process, simply lay the affected slime into a glass bowl until it forms back into one piece (approximately 3 minutes).

4. Now that you have your colors ready, tear the slime into strips, alternating colors. Lay the colored strands on your hand and let the slime drip down. Then put your hands together and stretch the colors out, twirling them into little towers of "unicorn poop." After playing for awhile, the slimes will start to combine to form a single color.

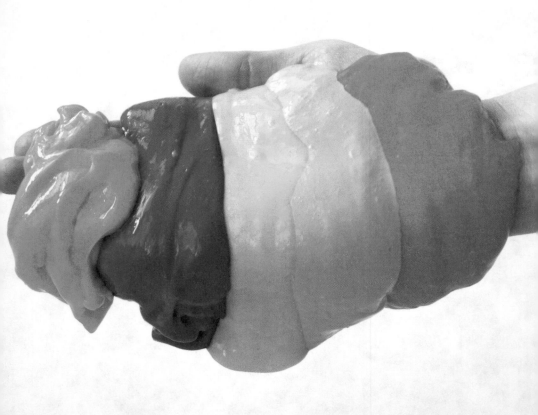

CARNIVAL SLIME

Consistency: Thick, Flows slowly

Dubbed carnival slime by my daughter and coauthor, Charlotte, this beautifully bold, striped slime is a combination of five separate colorful paint slimes. Because paint slime is stronger than regular white glue slime, this slime will also tear in half, bringing another experience to play time.

For each color in this slime, you will need:

- 1/2 cup white glue
- 1/3 cup liquid starch
- 2 teaspoons acrylic paint colors (Colors needed to duplicate: light pink, hot pink, red, blue, and orange)

INSTRUCTIONS:

1. For each color, measure out 1/2 cup of white glue and pour it into a cup or large bowl. Add two tablespoons of acrylic paint colors.

2. Add 1/3 cup of liquid starch into each bowl and combine. Your glue should start to form into slime almost immediately.

3. Pull out the slime and begin passing back and forth between your hands, stretching and kneading. If there

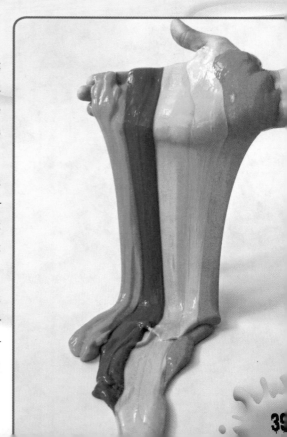

is any starch left in the bowl or cup you used, dip your slime back in to make sure it absorbs all of the remaining starch. This takes approximately 3–4 minutes.

4. Now take all five slime colors and lay them out flat on your hand. Lift your hand up and let the colors slowly start to drip down into stripes. Colors will eventually combine after a certain amount of play. Then you can knead and tear slime in half, or you can thin out and try to capture an air bubble inside the slime!

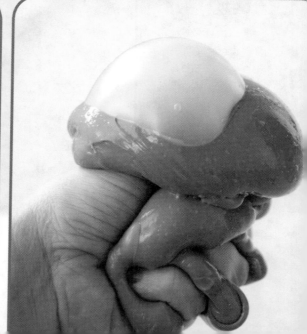

HEARTBEAT SLIME

Consistency: Thick, Flows slowly

After creating all of these slime combinations, you will have learned how to make paint slime, metallic paint slime, and white glue slime. Using the leftover slimes from previous projects, we combined 7 separate colors to create a slime that reminded us of a heart due to its coloring and appearance.

Colors we used:

- Yellow
- Red
- Light orange
- Dark orange
- Light pink
- Hot pink
- Teal
- Purple

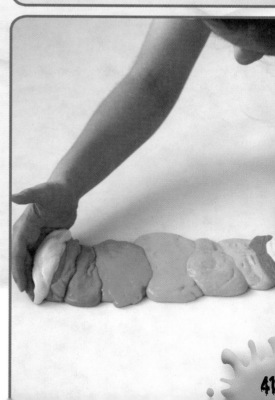

INSTRUCTIONS:

1. Lay your colors side by side on a nonstick vinyl, alternating strips of color. Pick the slime up in your hand, slowly folding it together.

2. Now, making sure the slime is stuck to the tips of your fingers, turn your hand upside down and let the slime flow. Every strip of color will look beautiful as it falls. Turn your hands around from side to side and see the waves of color fall down as you alternate. Slowly pick up the slime in your hand and do it again and again!

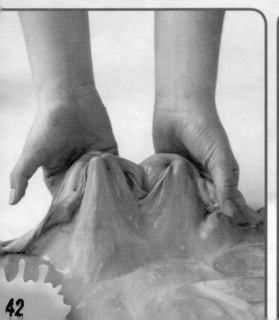

EXPERIMENT WITH SLIME

Making slime is only half the fun. Once you have created your ooey, gooey slime, there is so much more you can do with it! Incorporating slime into an experiment, passing it out as gifts, or seeing how long it can sustain its stretch and pull are only a few fun things that you can do with slime. On the following pages are a few other creative examples of slime activities and experiments.

BLOWING BUBBLES WITH SLIME

You would not believe how easy it is to blow a bubble with slime! To do this, simply take your slime outside, stretch it as thin as possible, take a big breath, and blow into the thinnest part.

How big you can make your bubble?

Note: Please keep this a safe distance from your mouth and do not ingest. Slime is not meant for human consumption!

TWO-PERSON BUBBLE

Want an even bigger bubble? This one takes two people. Create your slime and have each person grab an end and stretch out slowly. Once the slime has formed a sheet (careful, not too big or it will break!) slowly bend at the knees, bring your slime back up again to chest height, and pull it down quickly. Watch as the slime creates huge bubbles! This can easily be made into a game. Try again and again to see if you can beat the size of your previous attempt! Or compete against your friends!

JUMP ROPE WITH SLIME

Did you know you can jump rope with your slime? Test out a few recipes (white glue recipes work best). Once you are happy with your slime consistency, stretch it out and try to jump rope! Charlotte got two full jumps with hers.

DON'T TOUCH THE GROUND!

Taking at least two of your slime recipes, race them to the ground! How long does it take for each slime to reach? It's fun to try to get it closest to the ground without breaking. Our best length, so far, was 5'11".

Can you beat our record?

CRAFTING WITH SLIME

Slime also makes for some super fun crafting ideas! Here are a few that will show you how to use your slime in other innovative ways.

You make my heart melt

VALENTINE'S DAY CLASSROOM GIFTS

Slime is perfect to pass out as a Valentines Day gift! (This recipe can also be applied to Halloween.) Simply create your favorite slime recipe that's able to be stored (for example: red/pink slime using the white glue recipe for Valentine's Day or green snot slime for Halloween) and add to decorative bags to pass out. The slime keeps well when it's in a sealed container. You can make a large batch and separate into individual portions for a whole classroom, a team, or an activity group.

Adding a printed tagline like "You make my heart melt" is a perfect way to customize the message.

Note: Before passing out, please be sure to inform parents, teachers, classmates, and friends that slime is not edible!

EASTER EGGS

Instead of candy in your Easter eggs this year, fill them up with egg slime! Kids will love finding these special eggs in the yard or in their Easter baskets. (Again, be careful to remind them that it's not edible!)

For this project, you will need:

- Plastic Easter eggs
- White and yellow colored slime (See previous instructions for making white glue slime on pages 2-3)

INSTRUCTIONS:

1. Lay out small bits of white slime and add a tiny round yellow piece in the middle for the yolk. Let sit about 1 minute so it absorbs together.

2. Close the egg and hide it.

MASON JAR SNOWMAN

Not only are mason jars great for storing slime, but you can also decorate them in tons of adorable ways! Just take this mason jar snowman, for example. Easily made, this is a holiday decoration kids can help create and looks great on a shelf all season long.

For this project, you will need:

- Mason jar
- White glue slime (See previous instructions for making white glue slime on pages 2–3)
- Small styrofoam balls
- Decorating items for snowman's face

INSTRUCTIONS:

1. Create "snow" slime using the white glue recipe.

2. Mix in small foam balls, leaving some on the inside and the outside of the slime.

3. Put slime inside mason jar and seal.

4. Decorate the jar with a nose, hat, two eyes, and a mouth!

BIRTHDAY PARTY FAVORS

Slime is fun for everyone and makes a great "thank you" gift in goodie bags for birthday parties. In fact, it's also a fun activity for kids to do at a party!

INSTRUCTIONS:

1. Make your slime in a variety of colors and consistencies.

2. Add to condiment containers with lids.

Note: Any recipe that creates a storable slime works for this project!

MAD SCIENTIST

With all the ways slime can be made, it's an experiment in every recipe. Take it one step further by setting up a mad scientist's laboratory.

For this project, you will need:

- Vegetable oil
- Baking soda
- Snot slime (See previous instructions for making snot slime on pages 32-33)
- Vinegar
- Two jars (preferably beakers, if you want to stick to the theme)
- Food dye

INSTRUCTIONS:

1. Create your slime. (Green works best for this project.)
2. Mix your vinegar and a drop of green food dye.

3. Layer slime and baking soda in a jar at approximately the halfway point.

4. Slowly pour your green vinegar to the top of the jar and watch it bubble over.

5. Fill up second beaker with vegetable oil and slowly drop slime in to create an icky floating brain or add googly eyes to make a monster growing within.

SUN CATCHERS

Clear glitter slime looks beautiful when the sun shines through it! Create a sun catcher with a variety of colors and put in your window to use as a happy little decoration.

For this project, you will need:

- Shaped container with lid, needs to have separation between areas
- Clear glue slime (See previous instructions on pages 7–8)

INSTRUCTIONS:

1. Create a variety of translucent glitter slimes.

2. Put in a container shaped like a heart, flower, or rainbow.

3. Hang in a window or place it on a ledge near sunlight for a pretty sparkle.